World War I

When the Lights Went Out in Europe

Liam and Aoife's
Second Adventure

ROD SMITH

Published 2019
by Poolbeg Press Ltd
123 Grange Hill, Baldoyle
Dublin 13, Ireland
E-mail: poolbeg@poolbeg.com

Typesetting, editing, layout, design, ebook © Poolbeg Press Ltd.

A catalogue record for this book is available from the British Library.

ISBN 978-1-78199-7789

Typeset by Poolbeg Press Ltd

Cover illustrated by Derry Dillon

Printed by ScandBook, Lithuania

www.poolbeg.com

About the Author

Rod Smith was born in Drogheda. He lives in Malahide with his wife Denise, sons Alex and Oisín, and dog Sandy. This is his eleventh book, and his second historical novel. He is a graduate of Dublin City University where he holds a Bachelor of Arts (Hons) and a first class Master's Degree in Information Systems Strategy. He is currently studying for a Master's in Creative Writing at the Open University.

Dedication

To Denise – thanks for always being there

Contents

Illustration by Sara Dooley

Foreword

My name is Liam O'Malley. I am twelve years old. And thanks to the magical powers of my baby sister Aoife, I can time-travel! Honest! In my previous adventure with Aoife we travelled back in time and met Oliver Cromwell. Along the way we made some new friends who I will tell you all about in this story. This is our second adventure together. Join me now as I travel back to 1914 and the First World War!

Chapter 1

Present Day: The Hospital

We are running out of time. We are literally running out of time.

"Faster, Ferdia, faster! The darkness is closing in! Go! Go!" I know that if the darkness reaches us, we will be swallowed up in time and will cease to exist.

My horse Ferdia is running as fast as he can but I am not sure if we are going to make it. My luck may finally have run out. I may not get back from this adventure.

It is the month of November in the year 1918. We are racing across France and nearing the cliffs of Étretat in the north-west.

We approach the huge white cliffs. Ferdia is not slowing down.

"Whoa, Ferdia, whoa!" I shout as I pull back on the reins.

Ferdia ignores me and jumps off. As we dive into the sea, I hang on to his neck for dear life and clamp my legs to his back. The water is fast approaching. They say your life flashes before you at the end. I'm only twelve, so that doesn't last long. I think of my mother and my baby sister Aoife in hospital. I was there too. The water is getting closer and closer. Is this the end for me? I feel the cold water hit me with such a great force that I am thrown off my horse. We both are sinking down, down into the deep dark waters. It's getting hard to breathe. I can't get back to the surface no matter how hard I try. I am beginning to lose consciousness. I can see a purple light … what is it? I wish I were back where it all began …

🐴 🐴 🐴

I was still recovering in hospital after suffering an accident during a school history trip to Drogheda to learn more about Oliver Cromwell. I know, I know – how do you get hurt on a school history trip, I hear you ask? Well, a heavy cannon that was supposed to be chained up on a hill somehow broke free and came rushing towards me and my friends. I was pulled out of the way by the bus driver Mr Rafferty before it hit me, but the bang on the head I received from its rim knocked me unconscious. I spent six days in a coma before waking up.

During that time, I had an adventure in the 17th century with my sister Aoife and met Oliver Cromwell, Ferdia the horse, Seamus the pirate and Phelim the grumbling dockworker.

You believe me, of course. Don't you?

Anyway, here I am in my hospital bed, still recovering. My mum is in the same hospital! She has just given birth to my darling baby sister Aoife, so we are ward neighbours!

Time passes slowly in a hospital. There's nothing to do but rest and recover – and travel up and down in the elevators! Just don't let the nurses find you doing it! I have started to spend a lot of time visiting my mother and Aoife. It's funny, I never realised how little Mum and me talked to one another before the accident. Mum always wanted to talk to me, but I kept telling her I was too busy – going out to meet friends, looking at my apps, playing a video game, or watching television!

So here I am, off to visit my mum and new baby sister who is now just two days old.

"Good morning, my love!"

"Morning, Mum! Morning, Aoife!"

Aoife burped in response. Mum laughed.

"She's just had a full feed!"

"Well, better out than in!" I joked.

I heard a number of voices and a large commotion in the corridor outside.

"*Liam! Where are you, Liam?*" someone called.

I heard a girl's voice I recognised then.

"Stop shouting! There are people in here trying to rest."

"Pardon?" came a boy's voice.

"*I said stop shouting! There are people in here trying to rest!*"

"All right, all right, keep it down, no need to shout. You'll upset the patients. *OW!* Why did you pinch me?"

"I'm sure that's his mum's room," another voice said.

I popped my head out of the door.

"Hi, folks!"

"*Liam!*" they shouted as they piled into the room and hugged me.

Mum smiled. "Hello, Pat – Nuala – Mikhail – Sanjay!"

"Hello, Mrs. O'Malley!" they replied in unison.

"Hello, Aoife!" Nuala whispered as she bent over the cot.

Aoife's eyes were only half open.

Mikhail wheeled his wheelchair over to look. "Aah, I think she's just starting to doze off."

Pat smirked. "You better keep it down then, Nuala – you don't want to wake her!"

Nuala looked at Pat with dagger eyes.

"So what's new then, guys?" I asked to change the subject.

Pat groaned. "Mr. Clarke has us working on a new history project."

"Sounds exciting," I replied.

Sanjay laughed. "Says the person who doesn't have to do it!"

"What's the topic?"

Mikhail looked up from the cot. "The First World War."

Nuala nodded. "The war to end all wars."

"Then how come there was a Second World War?" Pat said mockingly and shrank back as Nuala advanced towards him menacingly. "All right, all right! Just trying to have a little joke. What's the matter with you all? Where's your Irish sense of humour?"

"I'm Nigerian!" Nuala replied.

"I was born in Bangalore!" Sanjay said.

"Is that somewhere in Kerry?" Pat asked.

Sanjay laughed. "Hey, even *you* know that it's in India!"

"Well, it looks like it's just you and me, Mikhail, to fly the Irish flag!" said Pat.

Mikhail removed his glasses and started to clean them as he frowned at Pat. "Don't tell me you've forgotten that I was born in Poland?"

"Of course he has!" said Nuala. "His brain is like a sieve – it can't hold on to any information."

"Look, we've all been living here for years so we're all half-Irish," Mikhail said.

"Oh yeah?" said Pat. "Well, I'm whole-Irish!"

5

"So what have you found out so far about the war?" I said, trying to calm the situation.

Mikhail took the hint. "It all started off with an assassination in Serbia."

"Yeah, Frank Ferdin Handy somebody," said Pat.

"Franz Ferdinand!" Sanjay said.

"Aren't they a band?" Pat asked.

"So how did that lead to a world war?" I asked, ignoring Pat.

Mikhail spoke again. "This is where it gets a little bit complicated."

"How?"

"Well, Franz Ferdinand was an Archduke and in line to become leader of the Austro-Hungarian Empire. He was shot in June 1914. Austria declared war on Serbia in July. Germany was an ally of Austria and joined in too. Russia supported Serbia, so Germany declared war on Russia. France was friends with Russia so Germany declared war on France. Then, when the Germans invaded Belgium in early August in order to circle around and attack France, Britain declared war on Germany."

Pat put his hands on his forehead. *"Information overload! My brain hurts!"*

"It's not used to learning stuff!" Nuala said.

"Why were they all in such a rush to go to war?" I asked.

"They all thought it would be over by Christmas," Nuala replied.

Mum interrupted. "They thought the war would be over in a few months. It lasted over four years."

"I didn't know you were a war expert, Mrs. O'Malley!" Sanjay said.

Mum didn't answer him. She was staring into space.

I noticed Sanjay was looking a bit embarrassed at her silence.

"Mum?" I said and touched her arm.

She looked at me, but it was as if she wasn't seeing me.

"He said he could have killed him, you know, but he didn't," she said. "He only wounded him."

I worriedly looked at Mum. "What do you mean, Mum?"

Mum closed her eyes for a few seconds and then seemed to come back to her senses.

"Oh nothing, nothing at all. Now why don't you all go down to the hospital restaurant and you can get a drink and a snack?" She took her red purse from under her pillow and opened it. "Here's some money."

Nuala reached out to take it. "Thanks, Mrs. O'Malley! Come on, guys!"

"Are you sure you're all right, Mum?" I asked.

"Yes, yes, I'm fine. Off you go now, children, and treat yourselves!"

Pat stood up on his tippy toes and pulled his shoulders back to make himself look taller.

"Actually Mrs. O'Malley, some of us are twelve and will be thirteen soon, so we will soon be technically 'young adults' or 'teenagers' and not 'children'."

Mum smiled. "Thank you, Pat, that's good to know. I'll see you later, Liam."

"Is your mum okay?" Nuala asked me discreetly as we walked down to the canteen.

"I think so."

"She seemed a bit upset there for a moment when she was talking about that person. Do you know who it was?"

I shook my head. "No, I don't."

When we got back to the ward Mum appeared to be still deep in thought.

"Mum, is everything all right?" I asked.

"Of course, Liam. Your chat earlier stirred some memories in me, that's all."

Pat sat on the side of Mum's bed, joined his hands together and looked earnestly at Mum.

"Would you like to talk about it, Mrs. O'Malley?" he asked.

Nuala shot a glance at Pat who chose to ignore her completely.

Mum laughed. "Thank you, Pat. Actually, I would. Well, you see, we used to call Liam's great-grandfather Tom Boyle 'the unknown soldier of the First World War'."

"Unknown?" I asked, puzzled. "Unknown to who?"

8

"'To *whom*'," said Nuala in a posh accent and I glared at her.

"Mrs. O'Malley," said Sanjay, frowning, "I thought our history notes said an Unknown Soldier was an unidentified soldier killed in a war who's buried and honoured as a representative of all the other unidentified dead soldiers?"

"You're quite right, Sanjay," said Mum. "We just called him that as a joke. But, let me explain. You see, when I was a child –"

"How long ago was that, Mrs. O'Malley?" Pat interrupted. "If you don't mind me asking?"

This time it was my turn to stare at Pat in disbelief.

"Sorry," he whispered.

Mum just smiled. "When I was a child, Tom used to come and visit us from time to time," she said. "He tended to sit in the corner and just stare out the window. He always seemed to have something on his mind. I often wondered what it was. He was a very quiet person who rarely spoke, unless it was to say the same line over and over. '*I could have killed him, but I didn't. I didn't. I shot him in the arm.*' The others used to laugh and say, 'Don't mind Tom! He's always going on about that!' One day I asked my older cousin, 'Who is he talking about?' My cousin sighed. 'Oh, some fellow he thinks he shot in the First World War! He thinks he fought in it – but he can't have – he was only fifteen when the war started. You had to be eighteen to join up and nineteen before you were allowed to fight overseas."

"So your grandad was delusional?" Pat said.

"Pat!" Nuala exploded.

"It's all right, Nuala," said Mum. "Pat, just let me tell you the rest of the story and you can judge for yourself. Well, one evening Tom was visiting – I think I was about your age – and when tea was being served Tom didn't come into the dining room. Mum asked me to go and find him. He was sitting outside in the garden just looking into space. 'Would you like to come in for your tea?' I asked. He looked at me for a moment and looked away again. 'Come on, Grandad – let's go in,' I said. 'I could have killed him,' he whispered. 'Who could you have killed?' I asked. He turned slowly towards me. I asked again, 'Who could you have killed, Grandad Tom?' There was a long pause. 'Geri,' he said – he always called me Geri – 'you are the first person to ever ask me that question. The others don't believe me when I say I fought in the Great War. They think there's something wrong with my memory, but there's not. Yes, I was too young to join up, but I was there!' He sounded really sincere. 'I believe you,' I said. 'Why don't you come in for some tea and afterwards you can tell me all about it?' He sighed. 'Well, I am a bit hungry. Do you have soft-boiled eggs?' I smiled. His teeth were not the best and with soft-boiled eggs he didn't have to chew.

'I'll ask Mum – she'll make some for you,' I said. Then he looked at me and said, 'I do still have my own teeth, you know. I keep them in a glass by the side of my bed!' I laughed and for the first time I saw a twinkle in his eyes as if he had come out of a deep muddle. But after tea I never got the chance to talk to him on his own."

"What happened then?" I asked.

"He passed away that same night after he went to bed. He died thinking that nobody believed him."

"Oh, no!" said Nuala. "That's so sad!"

"What a story he could have told," Mikhail said.

"Yes, I'm so sorry that I didn't talk to him that night – that I never took the time before that to sit and talk with him, really talk with him. I was always too busy with my friends, you see."

Pat nodded. "I know what you mean, Geri. Family is important."

Nuala sighed and threw her eyes up to heaven. "Come on, folks, let's go!"

"Thank you for sharing that with us, Mrs. O'Malley," said Sanjay politely. "Liam, I have something for you here …" He pulled some papers out of his backpack and handed them to me. "Here's some of the information on the war that we used for the project. I know you like history."

"That's not natural!" Pat joked. At least I think he was joking!

After they left, I sat there thinking about Mum's story and feeling guilty. I was always too busy on my phone or meeting with my friends. I never seemed to have the time to talk to my family. I read through some of the notes Sanjay had given me and fell asleep in the chair beside Mum's bed.

A short time later Mum tapped me on the shoulder. "I just need to go to the bathroom – will you watch over Aoife for me?"

"Yes, Mum."

When Mum was gone, I walked over to the cradle. Aoife's eyes were wide open and looking from side to side. They say new-borns can't see very well but I wasn't so sure in Aoife's case.

"Were you listening to Mum?" I asked her. "What do you think? Did our great-grandfather really fight in the First World War? What I would give to find out!"

As I stroked Aoife's soft head, I became aware of a tingling sensation that started to shoot through my fingers, up my arm, my neck and into my head. The room began to spin but I felt very relaxed. Then the room was filled with a very bright purple light. I shut my eyes tight and put my hands over Aoife's eyes.

Then there was the chatter of lots of people.

Chapter 2

1914: Great-grandfather
Tom and the First World War

A twelve-year-old Aoife stood beside me.

"Hello again, brother!" she said and laughed as she hugged me.

"Aoife, I haven't seen you this old since we met Cromwell!" I replied as I rubbed my eyes.

"What are you saying?" she joked. "That I look ancient? That's insulting!"

"Well, you know what I mean!"

We looked around.

"Where are we?" I asked.

"It's an army recruitment office in Dublin," she said. "Don't worry, nobody can see or hear us."

"What happened?" I asked.

Aoife pointed to a tall, dark-haired young guy who was whispering to a ginger-headed boy.

"You wished that you could find out if our great-grandfather fought in the war! Well, there he is, about to enlist!"

"So he did enlist! Oh, I'm not sure I want to see this!"

"You should be careful what you wish for then!"

We moved closer to the boys, to hear what they were saying.

The ginger-haired boy spoke first. "Well, Tom, are you still going through with it? I am if you are!"

"Of course I am, Jack! How else are we going to get Home Rule for Ireland? John Redmond believes that England will allow it after the war is over, so he says Irishmen should join the British army and support the war effort now."

I remembered from Sanjay's notes that John Redmond was a politician who wanted Ireland to govern itself rather than be governed by England.

The boy called Jack laughed. "Never mind Home Rule! I'm doing it for the adventure! Think of the places we'll be travelling to!"

"That's right!" Tom nodded. "We could end up in France or Belgium or even Turkey!"

An older man, a sergeant no doubt, was passing and overheard the conversation.

"Poor little Belgium!" he said, shaking his head. "Have you heard what the Germans are doing over there?"

14

"No, sir," Tom replied.

"They're killing innocent women and children with pitchforks!" he declared.

"The savages!" Jack shouted. "Belgium is a small country like ourselves – we have to defend them. It's the right thing to do!"

"That's not true, what they're saying about Belgium," I said to Aoife. "It's just propaganda being used to get people to join the war."

Aoife looked puzzled. "What's propaganda?"

"Spreading information that is not true to try and win support," I replied.

"You mean like telling lies?" she asked.

"Yes, I suppose so, if you put it like that," I said.

Jack and Tom were now walking over to join the queue of men looking to join the army.

Another sergeant, with a large bushy moustache, was directing the queue. "That's it, boys, right this way to volunteer! Come on and fight for King and Country!"

As they made their way to the top of the queue, both boys began to look anxious.

"Tom, are you sure we'll be accepted? We're only fifteen!"

"Of course we will – they're desperate for soldiers! The German army is much bigger than the British one. Come on, it's almost our turn!"

When they reached the desk at the front they were

spoken to by an old and craggy recruitment officer who also had a large bushy moustache.

"How old are you two lads?" he asked.

"Eighteen, sir!" they replied together nervously.

"I'm a sergeant. Don't call me sir! Good men. Well, sign here. You're a bit too young to go to the front just yet, but we'll train you for a few months and then send you off."

"Now what about your friend here?" the sergeant asked then, pointing directly at me.

I got such a shock. Aoife had said we couldn't be seen.

Tom grimaced and shrugged his shoulders. "He's not with me."

The officer looked at me closely. "Well, he looks like you – are you telling me the truth?"

"Of course I am – I've never seen him before!" Tom insisted.

The sergeant looked at me impatiently. "Well, cat got your tongue, lad?"

"Can you see me?" I asked, which was a stupid question with him staring straight at me.

"Well, of course I can! Did you leave your brains outside, young fella?"

"No, sir."

"So you want to enlist?" he said.

"Enlist? I don't know if –"

"You don't know?" he interrupted, glaring at me.

"You're a fine, tall, well-built chap – aren't you going to help your country in its time of need?"

A fine, tall, well-built chap? What was he talking about? I looked around. Aoife was now nowhere to be seen.

"Well ... I ... I ..."

"So what's it to be, lad? Come on – the queue is building up behind you."

I surprised myself when I blurted out, "Yes, I'm here to sign up, sir."

"Well done. Age?"

I hesitated for a moment. As I looked around the room for Aoife again, I caught sight of myself in a mirror. I looked much older! I even had some stubble on my chin! I couldn't believe it!

"I'm eighteen, sergeant!" I answered boldly.

"Of course you are!" the sergeant said with a smile.

Suddenly Aoife reappeared. "What are you doing?" she demanded.

"Where did you disappear off to?" I asked.

"What did you say, lad?" the sergeant asked.

"He can't see me!" Aoife said.

"Er, nothing, sir!" I replied nervously.

"Let's get on with it then. Stop wasting my time!"

An officer came over to us.

"Sergeant, what is going on here?"

"Nothing, sir. This brave young man is volunteering."

17

"Nonsense, man, he doesn't look old enough. Go home, lad, and come back in a couple of years!"

"Thank goodness!" Aoife sighed.

I looked at Tom sadly. He nodded at me sympathetically and went over to talk to Jack.

"How are they able to see me and why do I look older?" I asked Aoife.

She shrugged her shoulders. "Beats me! I'm only getting the hang of these time-travelling powers. Remember I'm still only two days old!"

I was stopped by another recruitment officer as I walked towards the door.

"Why so sad, young fella?"

"That officer won't let me enlist. He says I'm too young."

"Does he now? If you're willing to fight, it doesn't matter how old you are. Listen, the captain has gone off for his lunch now. Join that other queue and I'll have a word on your behalf with a different recruiting officer. We'll have you signed up in a couple of shakes of a lamb's tail!"

"Don't do it, Liam!" Aoife pleaded.

"I have to, I'm here for a reason," I replied.

Within a few minutes I signed up and was handed a silver coin.

I noticed Tom was still there with Jack. I walked over to him.

"So they let you in then!" Jack remarked.

"It was never in doubt," Tom said. "The recruitment officers have to get a certain number of volunteers every day. They get extra money as a bonus if they get additional people to join. It doesn't matter what age they are! What's your name, squirt?"

I winced. Who was he calling a squirt?

"I'm Liam," I said.

"Hi, squirt. I'm Tom Boyle. This is Jack Kennedy."

I ignored the insult.

"What's this for?" I held up the coin. I was trying to break the ice.

"Don't you know? That's the King's shilling! When you join the army the King gives you a shilling."

"How much is it worth?"

"Worth? What do you mean? It's worth a shilling of course! Or twelve pence."

"What's twelve pence?" I asked.

"You're a strange one, and that's no lie," Tom remarked, shaking his head.

"All right, you three, get over to the medical team pronto!" roared one of the sergeants. *"The doctors have to certify that you are fit to serve!"*

We went to another room where there was another queue of recruits, this time waiting to be seen by a number of doctors and some nurses.

"Go into one of those cubicles and take off your shirt, please," said a nurse.

I did as I was told.

"You will be seen by the doctor in a moment. Have you any illnesses to declare?"

"No."

I seemed to pass my tests without any problem.

I met Tom and Jack outside after the examination.

Jack was crying.

"What's the matter, Jack?" I asked.

"They said I'm not fit to serve. I have tuberculosis."

"What's that?" I asked.

"It's something to do with the lungs. They won't let me fight!"

Just then the sergeant we had been talking to appeared.

"Right then, all of you who have passed the medical, into the trucks now! It's off to training camp to teach you to become soldiers."

"Right now?" Tom asked.

"*Yes, on the double! You're soldiers now!*" the sergeant shouted.

Tom and I walked towards a truck that was waiting for us and climbed in. A dejected Jack stood beside the truck.

"So long, Tom!" Jack cried.

"See you, Jack!" Tom whispered. "Tell my mum I'm okay."

"I will."

The truck pulled away and Jack soon faded into the distance.

Tom put his head in his hands. "What have I done?" he wondered aloud.

I tried to be comforting. "We'll be all right."

"Listen, squirt, Jack has been my friend since I was a nipper. No disrespect, but I hardly know you."

"I know you better than you think," I replied.

"What do you mean by that?"

"Nothing."

Over the next few weeks we underwent military training. Aoife did not appear at all during this time. I wondered if she angry with me for volunteering. I tried to get close to Tom, but he kept his distance. It was almost as if he was blaming me for Jack's failure to join the army too.

Chapter 3

December 1914: Saint-Quentin, France

We didn't have to wait long to see real action. After some final training in England, we were told that we were to be transported by ship and train to France. As we boarded the ferry the reality of where we were and what we were doing really hit me for the first time.

"Does anyone know exactly where we're going?" I asked.

"Northern France, that's all we've been told," a voice mumbled. "Join the army and you'll see the world, that's what they told me. They never mentioned sea-sickness!"

"That will be the least of your troubles in the next few weeks," another voice in the darkness replied. "Wait until the fighting starts. Then you'll wish you were back on this boat!"

"How do you know?" I asked.

"I've been a soldier in the British Army for twenty years. I've had my share of battles," he replied.

"Why have you stayed so long in the army?" I asked.

"It pays a wage, lad. Thanks to the army, I can send money back to my family. There's no other work at home for people like me. I've always been a soldier and the army has taken care of me and my family. Now it's time for me to fight for the British Empire when it needs me most."

Another voice rang out. "The British Empire? What has it ever done for the Irish?"

"It has fed my wife and children and I won't hear a bad word said about the King or the Empire!"

"Spoken like a true Protestant!" the other voice said. "I take it you're from the North! I suppose the Unionist leader Edward Carson sent you?"

"I'm a Catholic!" the other voice replied. "And I'm from the South! I'm a Dubliner!"

An older voice joined in. "It doesn't matter whether you're Protestant or Catholic, North or South, we're all in the same fight and our blood is the same colour!"

The talking stopped after that.

I found this talk of Protestants and Catholics confusing. Looking up into the night sky, I tried to figure it out. 'Unionist' must mean someone who wanted Ireland to continue to be part of the United Kingdom . . . as Northern Ireland still is, even though the rest of the island is now a republic. And I knew there were lots of Protestants in Northern Ireland while the people in the South are mostly Catholics. It all began to make sense and I sighed to think that Ireland was so divided in 1914.

🐴 🐴 🐴

The crossing was smooth although a few soldiers got seasick due to the motion of the boat. One of them spent most of the journey with his head over the side being violently ill.

"I'm so glad we're on dry land!" he exclaimed after we had disembarked.

"Just as well you didn't join the navy!" another soldier joked.

"Tell me about it! I was so ill I thought I saw an animal swimming alongside us! Must have been a hallucination!"

"What kind of animal was it?" I asked.

"Well, don't laugh, but I could have sworn it was a horse! I've heard of sea horses, but this creature was bigger than I am!"

Everyone laughed except me. Something told me it had to be Ferdia, the horse who had saved me so many times during my adventures with Cromwell. I knew he wouldn't let me down!

We all boarded a train that was waiting for us.

I still had not seen Aoife since the day I had joined the army. I hoped that she was safe.

I settled down for the journey ahead.

"We'll be there just in time for Christmas!" someone joked as the train shunted along the track at a very slow pace.

"And then we'll have to turn back because the war will be over!" said Tom.

I remembered my mother saying that it lasted four years and my heart sank.

"Why do we keep stopping?" someone asked.

"They have to check the line for explosives, and make sure there is no enemy ahead," came the response.

When the train arrived at our destination, we all had to line up outside the station for inspection.

The seasick soldier I had spoken to earlier came towards me.

"Don't tell the others but I think I saw that same horse again, running alongside the train!"

"I believe you," I replied.

The soldier shook his head. "I must still be feeling the effects of the sea sickness!"

"That's got to be Ferdia," said a voice I recognised behind me.

I turned around and saw a boy in uniform. It was Aoife with cropped hair dyed black.

25

"Aoife! You're here! What happened to your lovely long brown hair?"

"I cut it short so that they wouldn't know I'm a girl. I can make them think I am older than I look too through the power of suggestion."

"I'm really glad to see you!"

"I will always be here for you, Liam, never forget that!"

I opened my arms to give her a hug.

"Better not – in front of all these people," she advised. "And my name's not Aoife! It's John!"

"John?"

"It's a very popular name in 1914!"

I stopped myself from laughing. "Fair enough, John! How does the uniform feel?"

"Itchy!" laughed Aoife, pulling at the material.

Aoife was right. Our dark khaki jacket and trousers were made from wool.

"Just wait until the weather gets warm – we'll be in such a sweat!" I joked.

"How are the boots?"

"A little big for me," she said.

"Put some newspaper in, that will help. They are quite heavy and stiff, aren't they? They're real leather with steel rivets, you know, to make them last longer."

"I only joined the army to get a new pair of boots!" a young soldier beside us commented after hearing our conversation.

I think he was deadly serious!

There was a lot of confusion at the train station. Nobody knew exactly where to go. A major selected a number of us to travel with his battalion. He was being tended to by a doctor.

"I'm Major Bridges. You people are to come with me. You are to be assigned to the Royal Irish Regiment. We'll take you along some of the way."

The doctor spoke. "Excuse me, Major Bridges, you have a concussion and a broken cheekbone. You should be resting."

The major was having none of it. "Nonsense, doctor, my legs are absolutely fine, so off we go!"

As we came near a town called Saint-Quentin, a man ran out and approached us.

"*Nous avons besoin de votre aide! Pas de combat, s'il vous plaît!*" he shouted in French.

"Does anyone know what he is saying?" Major Bridges asked.

Aoife nudged me. "You do."

"I do?"

"Yes, you do now. It's one of the powers I can give you – the ability to understand foreign languages."

I knew she had such powers.

"Excuse me, sir, I know some French," I told the major.

"Splendid. Can you translate? We can't afford to have any delays."

I walked up to the Frenchman who was very nervous and anxious and to my amazement was able to talk to him in French.

"What seems to be the trouble?" I asked him.

"Oh, thank goodness, you can understand me. I am the mayor of this town. I must ask you all not to fight. I do not want the town damaged or the people hurt."

"I do not know if that is possible – there is a war on, you know," I replied.

"But the other soldiers have agreed not to fight!"

"Other soldiers? What other soldiers?"

"Come in and see for yourselves. You will see that it is true!" And with that he turned around and walked back into the town.

I went back to the major and told him what had been said.

"Well, I sympathise with the mayor but he does not decide where or when the fighting takes place. What did he mean about other soldiers?"

"I don't know, sir – he says they're in the town now."

We marched into the town which was indeed packed with British Army soldiers sitting on the streets, in shop entrances and on the footpaths.

"What is going on here?" Major Bridges asked the

commanding officer who was sitting on a nearby wall.

"The men are too tired to fight," the officer replied. "We have written a message to the Germans who are coming, telling them that we will not oppose them."

The major was very angry. "What? You're surrendering?"

"We have been marching for days and have had very little food to eat. The men are in no condition to fight."

We looked around. Some of the men lying down on the street were sound asleep and snoring loudly.

"The people in the town took pity on some of them and gave them wine," the officer explained. "Drinking wine on an empty stomach is not a very good idea."

Major Bridges roared. *"All of you men, on your feet now! That is an order!"*

Nobody moved.

"We're not here to follow your orders!" a voice shouted out.

The major looked around and then pointed his finger at Aoife and me.

"You two!"

We looked at him. "Yes, sir?"

"I've got an idea. Come with me. We're going into that toy shop."

"Yes, sir!"

We marched into the shop to the surprise of the shopkeeper.

"*Parlez-vous* English?" the major asked.

The shopkeeper shook his head.

The major looked at me. "Ask him if he has got any drums or whistles."

The shopkeeper looked astonished when I asked the question. I must admit I was a bit taken aback too!

"Yes, monsieur, but I only have toy drums and toy whistles for children."

I translated the answer to the major.

"Tell him they will do very nicely," he commanded.

The major paid for a whistle and two drums and we walked out into the square. He handed a drum each to Aoife and me and kept the whistle for himself.

"Can either of you play the drums?"

"Yes, sir," I said. "Some friends and I have a rap group and we like to mess around with drum kits."

"What's rap?" Aoife asked.

"I'll tell you all about it when we get back!" I said.

The major laughed. "I'll never be up to date with you 1914 youngsters! Start beating that drum then."

I started to bang the drum. Aoife soon picked up the beat and joined in.

The major nodded. "Excellent, keep that up. Now we're going to march around the square. This music should get the soldiers back up on their feet. Follow me!"

The major led the way and started to play a marching tune on the toy whistle.

As we walked around, the soldiers who had been lying on the streets began to stir.

"*Come on, lads!*" the major urged as he stopped playing for a moment. "*March with me!*"

In the minutes that followed all of the soldiers picked themselves up and walked behind us. They all followed us safely away from the German army which was approaching from the other side of town. We stopped a few miles away at a meeting point where there were other army units.

The major was delighted with us. "Well done to you both!"

I smiled. "Thank you, sir!"

"You can really drum, boy! How long have you been playing?"

"I had a drum kit when I was younger, sir, and my mother always said there was a bit of a Ringo Starr about me!"

"What is a 'ringo star'?" Aoife asked.

"A person! He was one of the Fab Four – the Beatles! Best band ever, Mum says."

Aoife looked at me blankly.

"You are a funny chap, Liam!" the major said with a laugh. "I'll have to check out this Bingo Stark when I get home!"

"Ringo Starr, sir!"

We were interrupted by the arrival of two trucks.

"These trucks are for you and your companions," the major explained. "We'll part company here. You are going to meet up with your regiment. I hope we meet again in more peaceful times."

"So do I, sir," I replied.

We boarded the trucks that were waiting for us and set out on the next step of our journey.

"Wait! Where's Tom!" I shouted as I sat beside Aoife.

She pointed. "It's okay. He's on the truck behind us."

Night was falling as we left Saint-Quentin.

"We're heading north," Aoife said.

"How do you know?" I asked.

"From the stars," she replied.

I looked up at the night sky and thought of Mum back at the ward.

I must have dozed off because the next thing I remember was getting a nudge from Aoife.

"We're here."

I rubbed my eyes. "Where are we?"

"Neuve Chapelle," she replied.

Chapter 4

Christmas 1914: Neuve Chapelle,
France, and Captain Amos

A captain addressed us after we disembarked from the lorries. He was a handsome fit-looking man with a neat dark moustache – and not very old, it seemed to me. Something about him commanded respect. We all listened attentively.

"Welcome to Neuve Chapelle. I am Captain Arthur Moore O'Sullivan. You are all now part of the Royal Irish Rifles. For those of you who are curious, we are near the Belgian border and about 230 kilometres north of Paris. Most of you have never been in a battle situation before. It will be tough and there will be challenges. Remember, we are in this together and, God willing, we will all come through this alive and well. Now I will hand you over to the sergeant who will give you some important advice that may save your life."

Neuve Chapelle. Was there a battle here in the First World War? I didn't know. It wasn't mentioned in Sanjay's notes.

My thoughts were interrupted by a burly sergeant who started to speak.

"Now listen up! If you pay attention, these three rules may just save your life! Rule Number 1 – keep your heads down at all times. We don't know how many enemy snipers are out there, just waiting for you to show your noggin!"

"Noggin?" I asked.

"Your head, lad!" the sergeant roared. "Rule Number 2 – when you're smoking do not light up at night. The snipers will see the flame and try and shoot you. Rule Number 3 – if you disobey rule Number 1 or rule Number 2 and get yourself shot, I will wring your bloody necks! If you get shot, I will have to fill out a lot of forms. I do not like filling out forms! Is that understood?"

"Yes, sergeant!" they all replied.

"Excuse me, sergeant," I said, "but if we disobey the first two rules, we'll probably be dead.

"Correct. What is your point?" the sergeant barked back.

"Well, if we're dead, why wring our necks?"

"It will make me feel better!" he roared as he marched away with the captain who was grinning at my question.

34

I shook my head as the sergeant left. A soldier beside us lit a cigarette.

"We're allowed to smoke? That's crazy!" I said to Aoife who was standing beside me.

"Why?" asked Tom, at last speaking to me.

"Well, smoking is so bad for you. It's a health hazard!"

Everybody looked at me in amazement and then started to laugh and jeer. Even Tom joined in.

Aoife and I looked around, confused.

A voice rang out.

"Oi! You lot! Have you nothing better to do? Go on, get out of it! Clear off!"

The soldiers jumped to attention.

"Yes, corporal!"

The corporal came over and put a sympathetic arm on my shoulder. His helmet was low over his forehead and his head bent.

"Don't mind them, lad. They're only having a joke at your expense. Smoking is the least of their problems. A lot of the lads here smoke to help pass the time. It can get very cold and very boring. It relieves the monotony."

That voice! It was so familiar!

The corporal raised his helmet so I could see his face.

"Seamus!" I shouted and then dropped my voice. "What are you doing here? I haven't seen you since our adventures with Oliver Cromwell!"

"It seems like only yesterday, lad!"

"Are you still a pirate?"

"Oh no, I've left those days behind me!" He pointed to his uniform. "I'm a corporal now – look – two stripes!"

"Seamus!" Aoife stepped up and gave Seamus a big hug.

"Ah, Aoife! A pleasure as always. What have you got us into this time?"

"I wish I knew, Seamus!"

"All we need now is Phelim," I said.

Seamus shook his head. "Don't ruin the moment now, lad. That old misery guts is always moping around somewhere!"

A soldier walked out of one of the shelters and looked directly at me.

"My ears are burning – is someone talking about me?" he asked.

"*Phelim!*" Aoife screamed and she and I ran to hug him.

Phelim looked at the two of us. "It's great to see you both but I have to say I'm not happy to see you here. There are better places than this."

"But how did you get here?" I asked.

"No idea, lad. All I know is that whenever you go on one of your time-travel jaunts it seems I am here to watch over you."

"Same for me!" Seamus added.

Phelim threw his eyes up to heaven. "Well, unfortunately we don't get to choose the company we keep!"

I laughed. "Good to see you two haven't changed anyway."

"So why are you here?" Phelim asked.

I pointed over to Tom. "I'm here with that chap over there. He's my great-grandfather."

"Well, he does have your big ears and stubby nose!" Seamus joked as he looked over at Tom who was busy cleaning his rifle.

"He's my relation too!" Aoife protested.

"Get out of that one, Seamus!" Phelim roared.

Seamus paused for a moment. "Well, big ears mean you must be a great listener!"

Aoife shook her head.

"Have you seen Ferdia?" I asked Phelim.

Phelim shook his head. "I haven't seen that old nag in ages. He'll show up when you need him. You can be sure of that!"

"Or when there's food to be had!" Seamus joked.

"One of the soldiers told Liam he'd seen a horse swimming next to the ship as they came here," said Aoife, "and then running by the train track."

"That'll be him," said Phelim.

"Speaking of food," said Seamus, "what's on the menu tonight?"

Phelim rummaged around in a kitbag lying nearby. "The usual," he said. "A nice tin of bully beef."

"What's bully beef?" I asked.

Seamus groaned. "It's corned beef in a tin and I'm sick to death of it."

"But we've also got some hard biscuits and stale bread," Phelim said, "and to top it off a nice hot drink which they'll be bringing up to us from the army kitchen. We always enjoy that, don't we, Seamus?"

"Can't wait." Seamus rolled his eyes. He turned to me. "Have you met Amos yet?"

"Who is Amos?" I said.

"That's Captain O'Sullivan. His full name is Arthur Moore O'Sullivan – A–M–O–S – Amos! Everyone calls him by that name."

"Yes, we've met him," Aoife said. "He spoke to us when we first arrived. He's a very impressive man."

Just then some of the kitchen staff arrived and distributed the hot drinks Phelim had talked about.

"Enjoy your tea!" Phelim said with a grin.

I raised the small tin containing the tea and took a big gulp of it.

"It tastes like vegetables!" I said, spluttering. "It's horrible!"

"That's because they make it in the same big vats where they make the stews … when they have ingredients to make stew," Seamus said with yet another sigh.

I decided I didn't care. I was so thirsty, I drank it anyway.

Later that night I joined Phelim on sentry duty.

"It will be Christmas tomorrow," Phelim said to me as I stood with him on sentry watch in the trench while the others slept.

"This is not the way I would choose to spend Christmas Eve!" I said as I stood in muck and pools of water. "My feet are soaking!"

"Sit down, lad," Phelim instructed. "Take off your boots and socks."

"Why?"

"Just do it."

I found a dry spot to sit down and did as he said.

Phelim handed me a bottle. "It's whale oil. Rub it into your feet. It will help you to avoid getting trench foot."

"Trench foot?"

"You get it from standing in water in the trenches all the time. Your wet feet go numb and gangrene can set in. You could lose a foot! Or feet! Where are your puttees?"

"My whatties?"

"To protect your legs!"

"I don't know what you're talking about!"

"It's like a long bandage that gets wrapped tightly around your legs and ankles and goes up to your knees. It's supposed to protect you against the damp, though I'm not so sure it does any good. I keep a spare pair in my kit bag for emergencies. Here, take them."

He took them out and handed them to me. I wrapped them tightly around my legs as instructed.

"Thanks, Phelim, that feels much better," I said gratefully.

"*Shush!*" Phelim raised a finger, listening. "Do you hear someone calling?"

We both strained our ears to listen.

"It's coming from the German side!" I said.

"*Can you hear us? Hello, can you hear us?*"

The words were being spoken with a German accent.

I shouted back. "*Yes, we can hear you!*"

"Hush, it might be a trap!" Phelim warned.

The voice continued to speak.

"*It is Christmas Eve. Do not shoot tonight or tomorrow and we will not either!*"

Seamus arrived, rubbing his eyes as he had just woken up.

"What's all this hullabaloo?"

"It's the Germans," I replied. "They're offering a Christmas truce!"

The voices continued and we could hear Christmas carols being sung in German. Some of our own squad began to sing in English in response.

"If you come out and talk to us, we will not fire!" The German voice repeated.

"It's definitely a trick!" Phelim declared.

"I don't think so! I've read about the famous Christmas truce! They're not going to shoot!" I shouted as I jumped up out of the trench and made my way across no man's land to the German trench.

Fortunately, nobody fired any shots.

When I reached the German side, I was met by a German soldier who handed me a cigar.

"Merry Christmas!" he said in perfect English.

"Merry Christmas to you too!" I replied.

"Where are your comrades?"

"Here we are!" shouted Seamus and Phelim who came running to my side.

"Smoking is bad for you – I'll take that cigar, thank you very much!" Seamus said as he grabbed the cigar from my hand and eyed it eagerly.

Soon soldiers from both sides climbed out of their trenches and met in the middle of no man's land.

"We thought this war would be over by Christmas," one of the German soldiers remarked.

"So did we!" Phelim replied.

"That's what happens when a bunch of old politicians send a bunch of young people off to fight a war on their behalf," Seamus moaned.

"We're not even sure what exactly we're fighting for!" Aoife said.

"We wonder that ourselves sometimes," the German soldier replied.

"So what happens now?" I asked.

By this time, Captain O'Sullivan had climbed out of the trench as well. He called us all to attention.

"We'll agree that there will be no shooting until the end of Christmas Day. Then I will fire a single shot to signify that the truce is over. So until then, make the best of it!"

"This is great!" I said.

Aoife nodded her head in agreement.

"Enjoy it while it lasts," the captain sad. "I don't think the generals will let us do this again!"

"Why not?" I asked.

"Because they'll be afraid that the soldiers won't shoot somebody that they've been singing and sharing sweets with."

Phelim's eyes started to bulge. "Who is sharing sweets?"

"Over there," I said, pointing to a group of Irish and German soldiers.

"*Hold on there, fellas! Keep a sweet or two for me!*" Phelim shouted as he ran in their direction. "*Have you got any chocolate?*"

Seamus shook his head. "I've never seen the old goat

run so fast in his life. Anything for a few chocolates!"

Phelim came back with his hands full of delights. "Very generous, very generous indeed!"

Seamus looked at them greedily. "Wait a minute. Did the German soldiers just give those to you? Without a trade?"

Phelim nodded and started to munch the sweets. Seamus took off to the other trenches in pursuit of something similar.

"Look at him!" Phelim roared. *"I've never seen the old turkey run so fast in his life!"*

"It's funny how goats and turkeys seem to like sweets!" I joked.

"What's that?" Phelim asked, not realising that the joke was on him.

"Oh, nothing!" I replied.

A German corporal walked over to me.

"Happy Christmas! My name is Helmut."

"Yes, Happy Christmas to you too. I am Liam. This is Phelim, John and the chap running back with the sweets is Seamus."

"I am very pleased to meet you all."

"Who is this John chap you're talking about?" Phelim whispered to me.

"Aoife!" I whispered.

Phelim winked to show that he understood.

"You speak English very well, Helmut," I remarked.

43

"Oh yes, I spent many years in Dublin studying at Trinity College."

"I'm from Dublin!" I said.

"What is an Irish chap like you doing fighting in this war?" Helmut asked.

"Fighting for the right to Home Rule!" Tom shouted as he joined the group.

"Home Rule? Do you really think the English will let you govern yourselves after this war?" Helmut asked.

"John Redmond promised us it would happen!" Tom replied.

"It's easy for the politicians to make the promises when they are not on these fields of death," Helmut argued.

"I like the buttons on your coat," I said, trying to change the subject as I could see Tom getting angry at what Helmut was saying.

"You like my buttons? Would you like one? Perhaps we can do a swap? I will take one of your buttons and you can have one of mine. It can be what you call a memento, yes?"

"Sure," I agreed.

Helmut produced a small penknife and cut off a button at the bottom of his coat.

"Don't worry! I have some spares!" he said with a laugh as he handed it and his knife to me.

There I was, facing an enemy who would have tried

to kill me just minutes beforehand. Now I was using his knife to remove a button from my coat.

"Have you any family waiting for you at home?" I asked.

"I have a wife and son. Would you like to see their picture?"

"Of course."

Helmut placed his hand in his inner coat pocket and produced a small brown wallet.

"This is the latest letter from home, with a picture. Look!"

He showed us a black-and-white photograph of a young woman holding a baby.

"You have a lovely family," I said.

"Yes, I am a very lucky man. What about you? Have you anyone waiting for you?"

"Yes, my mother and my baby sister."

"They must be worried about you."

"It's a bit complicated, but yes, yes, I suppose they are."

Helmut sighed. "There is nothing in the world more important than family. Never mind the politicians and the generals who want their wars. Family is what binds us all together."

I looked wistfully at Aoife. She had tears in her eyes.

"Nice chap," Phelim remarked as Helmut moved on to another group to share stories and chocolates.

"Makes you wonder why we're fighting them in the first place," Seamus replied. *"Ow!"* he roared as something hit him on the back of the head.

"Are you all right – have you been hit?" I asked, afraid that the ceasefire was over already.

"No – look!" said Aoife.

We were amazed to see a football at our feet.

"Who kicked that football!" Seamus roared as he rubbed his head.

A group of English soldiers roared at us. *"Come on! Let's have our ball back! The Germans are winning one-nil!"*

"Now, where did they find a football in the middle of all of this carnage?" Phelim asked.

"That's the wrong question!" Seamus insisted. "How can they be expected to shoot a gun properly when they can't even shoot a football straight?"

He bent down to pick up the ball.

"Get ready, lads, the Irish are coming! We'll show you how to play football properly!" he roared as he kicked the ball back and ran to join the game.

"He's wasting his time," I said. "The Germans will probably win in the end on penalties."

"What do you mean?" Phelim asked.

"Oh!" No penalty shoot-outs then of course. "Never mind. You wouldn't understand!"

Phelim laughed. "Well, get in there, young 'un, and help Seamus out. Are you coming, Tom?"

"No, I'm not playing games with the enemy. We're here for one thing and that's to kill as many of the Germans as we can!"

"So much for the Christmas spirit!" Phelim muttered as Tom stomped away.

♞ ♞ ♞

We spent the rest of the day playing football, sharing food and drinks and talking about one another's families.

Captain O'Sullivan issued the order to us as the night drew to a close.

"Right, lads, that's it now, back to the trenches!"

The sides separated and began to walk slowly back to their own trenches. Nobody wanted the day to be over.

As we settled back in the trenches, a shot rang out from Captain O'Sullivan's pistol to signal that the ceasefire had now ended.

"Keep your heads down lads, it's all over!" he commanded.

Just then a group of German soldiers appeared at the edge of our trench.

"Come on out!" they pleaded. "We have more chocolates!"

"Go on back to your own trenches now – the ceasefire is over!" the captain shouted.

The soldiers reluctantly turned back. The rest of the night passed peacefully.

Captain O'Sullivan was right. When the generals found out about the ceasefire, they sent out strict instructions that such a thing was never to happen again.

"I told you they would be against it!" Seamus said.

"Not the proper thing to do during a time of war!" Phelim agreed.

"We're here to kill, not to engage in pleasantries!" Tom declared.

Seamus looked at Tom and shook his head. "You really are a laugh a minute, aren't you?"

♞ ♞ ♞

A few months later, in March 1915, orders came that we were to go over the top and carry out a surprise attack on the Germans.

Phelim shook his head. "They want us to go after the same people who were playing football with us and sharing food and drink only a few months ago."

"Besides – it's suicide!" Seamus objected.

"We'll have some artillery cover during the attack," Captain O'Sullivan explained.

"Great, so if the Germans don't get us, our own artillery will!" Seamus moaned.

"Now who's a laugh a minute?" Phelim sneered.

"Fix bayonets! The artillery will be starting any time now. Wait for my whistle," Captain O'Sullivan ordered.

The captain took Aoife and me to one side before the attack.

"Now then, you two, could I have a quick word?"

I became very worried. Did the captain know something?

"Yes, sir," I replied nervously.

"This will be your first major battle. I want you to be stretcher-bearers. There are going to be a lot of wounded soldiers who will need your help. Are you up to the task?"

"Yes, sir!" Aoife and I replied in unison.

I breathed a sigh of relief. We would be both much happier trying to save lives than trying to take them.

"Of course, you haven't had any training in first aid unfortunately –"

"Excuse me but we have, sir!" I interrupted. "At Scouts, sir."

"Excellent. You'll be given a medical kit, though normally your job will be to get the wounded back to the medical unit as quickly as possible. Go back to the medical unit now and collect the kit and a stretcher."

The shelling began and lasted for about thirty minutes. Just after 8 a.m. the captain blew the whistle and the first wave of soldiers raced over the top, firing as they ran towards the enemy trenches. After what seemed like an eternity the shooting stopped.

Aoife and I grabbed our stretcher and went over the top to look for the wounded. The ground was covered with the bodies of the dead and the dying. The young soldier who joined to get a new pair of boots had been shot through the head. Phelim was standing beside him.

"Poor lad was killed as soon as he went over the top," he said sadly.

Aoife and I looked around. This was not an adventure. This was mass slaughter. I stood there in shock, feeling helpless. All I could do was say a prayer for the poor lad lying in this field of devastation.

Seamus and Tom arrived on the scene.

Tom's eyes lit up when he saw the dead soldier.

"That's a grand pair of boots. It would be a pity to let them go to waste!" He knelt down and started to remove the boots from the dead man.

"Leave him alone! They're his boots! He deserves to be buried with them!" I shouted.

Tom stopped what he was doing and stared at me.

Phelim intervened. "Some of our lads got as far as the German machine guns. Come on. Let's see if anyone needs our help."

The layers of barbed wire ahead of us had been partially destroyed by the shells. Groups of Indian soldiers lay dead or dying. We did what we could to make them comfortable but there was nothing else we could do except watch them die.

"Why is the Indian army here?" Tom asked.

"India is still part of the British Empire," I explained. "They are under British rule and agreed to send troops over to assist."

"Poor lads – they are part of the Indian Meerut Division that led the charge," Seamus said. "I hear the Indian Army provided half of the attacking force today."

"They were very brave," Aoife replied.

"Over a million of them will end up fighting this war," I said, remembering having read that – in my other life.

"It won't be won without their help," Phelim said.

When we reached the German lines we discovered that the German troops had retreated. The trenches were empty.

"Let's make sure there's nobody left hiding," Phelim suggested.

We searched everywhere, but there was no doubt. They were all gone apart from two lying face down in the mud.

Seamus went over to them. They appeared to be dead.

"Poor devils – it must have been the shrapnel from the shells. They didn't have a chance."

He turned the first body over. It was the soldier who

had struck the football against him only months previously. His legs had been blown off by the shrapnel.

Tom sneered. "He won't be hitting you again with a football anytime soon."

Seamus looked at Tom with a look of disgust and pity.

"He had a mother, just like you."

"What about the other person?" I asked fearfully.

Phelim turned him over. It was Helmut.

Seamus put his hand on my shoulder. "I'm sorry, lad."

I dropped to my knees and felt sick to the stomach.

"No visible wounds," Seamus said. "I wonder what killed him?"

Tom bent over and started to search his pockets.

"What are you doing?" I asked.

"He might have some more chocolates. He won't need them where he's going."

I jumped to my feet. Phelim restrained me.

"Get away from him, leave him alone!" I roared.

"Why are you so upset? He would have killed you if he had the chance!"

Tom continued to search his pockets and found the wallet containing the last letter from his wife and the photograph.

Tom threw them at me. "No chocolates after all. Here, you take this, seeing as you were such close friends!"

Phelim kept a tight hold of me.

"Don't do anything rash now, Liam," he whispered.

"How could we be related?" I asked. "He is so cold, so heartless!"

"War does strange things to people, it changes them."

"*Stop!*" Aoife shouted at Tom. "I think I saw him move!"

Aoife was right. The soldier's hand moved slightly and he spoke in a whisper.

"*Give me back my photograph …*"

"*Help him! He's still alive!*" I shouted.

Tom pulled out a small knife from his coat and raised it over the soldier's chest. "Not for long! This is for all of those women and children you butchered in Belgium. *Die, you filthy Hun!*"

Aoife yelled and jumped in front of Helmut while I threw myself at Tom and tackled him to the ground. We rolled around the mud as I desperately fought to stop him stabbing the injured soldier.

Seamus and Phelim stepped in to separate us.

Captain O'Sullivan appeared at the top of the trench. "What's going on here?"

"We've found a wounded German soldier, sir!" I replied, still gasping for breath.

"Use your stretcher! Take him to the medical unit!" he ordered as he climbed down. He looked squarely at Tom who still had his knife in his hand. "We're not murderers here. This man is a prisoner of war!"

"Come on, let's take him," I said.

Aoife and I laid our stretcher down by the stricken soldier, then Phelim and Seamus lifted him onto it. He was dazed but did not seem to have any bullet wounds.

Aoife looked at Tom. "Aren't you forgetting something?"

"What?"

"An apology for your behaviour!"

Tom stormed off in disgust.

"Here you are, Helmut," I said as I pressed the wallet into his hand.

"Ah, the Button Boy and friends," he whispered. "I did not expect to see you all again so soon."

"Don't talk now – we're going to get you some help."

We carried him off to the nearby medical unit which was an old school that had been abandoned because of the war.

"Please! We need some help here!" Aoife shouted as we approached.

A male attendant appeared at the door. "A German?" he said, noticing the German uniform. He pointed at a medium-sized tent outside. "Take him in there. We'll get a doctor to see him when one is available."

I was not having any of it. *"He needs a doctor now!"* I shouted.

A nurse appeared from inside the tent.

"What's the meaning of all the shouting here?" she demanded.

"This man needs to be seen now!" I pleaded.

"He's German," the male attendant mumbled.

"It's doesn't matter what side he is on. We are here to help the wounded," the nurse insisted.

"Very well, Nurse Cavell," he said.

"Don't worry," the nurse said to us. "I'll make sure he is well taken care of."

"Excuse me, are you Edith Cavell?" I asked, thinking back to Sanjay's notes again.

"Why, yes, I am. Do I know you, young man?"

"No, but I know you!"

"How, may I ask?"

"You're famous!"

She looked amused. "Certainly not. Now, I need to get on with training these nurses – I'm here for just a short time. Bring the soldier into the tent and we'll get him seen to."

Inside the tent, two doctors and another nurse were tending a large number of wounded men.

One of the doctors directed us to lift Helmut off the stretcher and onto a long table.

"You can go now," Nurse Cavell said. "Come back tomorrow. He's in good hands."

Seamus and Phelim picked up our stretcher and we all went outside.

Aoife touched my hand. "Don't worry, Liam – he'll be all right. I promise."

All of the horrors of the war seemed to engulf me at that instant and I burst into tears.

Aoife hugged me. "It's all right. I'm here for you."

"You have seen things a child should never have to see," Seamus said.

"No human being should ever have to witness this," Phelim added.

Aoife stroked my hair. "Come on, we've done all we can for Helmut. Let's see if there is anyone else who needs our help."

♞ ♞ ♞

On a later trip back to the medical unit we found Helmut still in the tent. He was lying on a thin mattress on the ground, and clearly much improved.

"You saved my life," he said to me, holding out his hand to shake mine.

"How are you feeling?" I asked as I shook it.

"Glad to be alive! No serious injuries. The blast from a nearby shell knocked me unconscious. I'll be all right in a couple of days."

"I just hope you get to see your wife and family again soon."

"Well, the war is over for me now. I will live to see the end of it even if it is in a prisoner-of-war camp. Perhaps we will meet again someday in happier times?"

"I hope so."

"I will never forget you, my saviour the Button Boy! There is something about you I cannot quite figure out. I think that perhaps you were meant to be there to save me!"

He was probably right! "I'm glad I was there to help."

And with that we said farewell.

We met Nurse Cavell on the way out.

"Will you be here for much longer?" I asked.

"No, I'm going back to Belgium where there are a lot of people who need my help."

"To escape from the Germans?" I asked.

She looked startled for a moment and then smiled. "Well, well, that's twice now you have caught me out. How did you know I help soldiers to escape? Are you a spy trying to catch me out?"

"No, no!" I protested. "I'm an admirer!"

"How charming!" she laughed and kissed me on the cheek.

I blushed as she walked away.

"She is a very brave lady," Aoife said. "Liam, why are you turning red?"

"Never mind that. What about Tom?" I asked, trying desperately to keep my composure.

"Well, at this stage, we know for sure that he really went to war," Aoife said.

"He's a monster! He was going to kill Helmut without a second thought. He is evil!"

"He's our great-grandfather!"

"That doesn't mean I have to like him!"

Seamus came over to me. "Sorry, lad – you and Tom have to report to the company lieutenant. Word about the skirmish between the two of you has been doing the rounds."

Tom and I went to the lieutenant's tent, accompanied by Seamus.

"Now then, it appears that you two were involved in a skirmish in the trenches. I will not tolerate such action in this unit. Would either of you care to explain what took place?" the lieutenant asked.

Tom began to look concerned.

I stepped forward.

"It was my fault, sir. We had a disagreement over something, and I attacked Tom."

"What was the disagreement about?"

"I'd rather not say, sir. It was a private matter."

The lieutenant looked at Tom. "Have you anything to say on this matter?"

Tom looked down at the floor in shame. "No, sir."

"Very well then. I will not tolerate such actions. It smacks of a lack of discipline. We have enough problems fighting the enemy without having to fight amongst ourselves. O'Malley, I admire your attitude in

58

taking responsibility for this, but acts like this must be punished. I sentence you to two days Field Punishment Number One."

Seamus tried to intervene.

"Begging your pardon, sir, but this is the first time he has come to your attention for this kind of behaviour."

"Noted, and that is why he is only getting two days, instead of a week. Carry out the punishment immediately, corporal."

Seamus nodded. "Yes, sir."

"What's Field Punishment Number One?" I asked as we left the tent.

Phelim and Aoife were waiting for us outside.

Tom looked at them and walked off, shaking his head.

"It means you're going to be tied to the wheel of one of the main guns for a few hours each day," Seamus replied.

Aoife started to protest. "But that's horrible!"

"Sorry, but that's the army way," Seamus replied. "I don't like it any more than you do."

"We'll try to make it as comfortable as we can for you," Phelim added.

They walked me up to one of the big guns which was positioned on a hill.

"Sit down there, lad," Phelim said as he produced some rope. "Don't worry, this gun won't be fired. It's not working properly."

"That's reassuring," I replied.

59

My wrists were to be tied to the wheel of the gun.

"Let's make sure these knots are not too tight," Seamus said to Phelim.

"You can slip your hands out when nobody is looking," Phelim said to me, "and slip them back in again when anyone comes near."

"Are you going to leave him here on his own?" Aoife asked as they started to walk away.

"We're not allowed to stay," Phelim replied.

I tried to reassure Aoife. "It's all right, Aoife – you go on now. I'll be fine."

Aoife kept looking back at me as they left.

"I'm okay," I mouthed.

To be honest, I felt quite scared. What if I was hit by a stray bullet or attacked by a wild animal? There I was, sitting in darkness, looking up at the stars in the sky, tied to the wheel of a gun. There was one star in particular that seemed to stand out from all of the others. Was it the strange star that had followed me during my time with Cromwell? I almost thought I could hear my mother's voice calling me. I shook my head. I was very tired and was probably imagining things. My stomach started to rumble. I hadn't eaten anything all day.

I decided not to pull my hands out of the ropes in case that got Seamus and Phelim into trouble.

I woke up the next morning cold and hungry. My whole body was aching. As the sun rose I was feeling very sorry for myself. I was visited by Tom and Aoife. They had brought some food.

Aoife ran towards me and knelt beside me.

"I came last night with some food and a blanket but the stupid sentry on duty wouldn't let me go near you!"

"You must be starving," Tom said, handing me some bread. "Sorry, it's a bit stale. It's all we could find."

"'*Hunger is the best sauce*'," I replied as I tried to force a smile.

I wolfed the bread down.

"Take your time, you'll make yourself ill!" Aoife warned.

Tom sighed. "Look, I'm not very good at saying sorry, but thanks for what you said to the Lieutenant last night."

"That's okay."

"No, it's not. What I did was unacceptable. Ever since I arrived here in France I've been a different person, a person I don't recognise, a person I don't like."

"They say war does that to people," I replied.

"How can you be so calm about all of this?" Tom said.

"I'm not calm. I'm scared."

"You? Scared? I don't believe it!"

"Anyone who says he is not scared is lying. Despite

that, I have a feeling that things will work out for all of us."

"What makes you think that?"

Aoife piped up. "Because we have people looking out for us!"

"Who is looking out for me?"

I looked into his eyes. "We are all looking out for one another."

Tom started to cry. Aoife joined in too, and then I began to cry.

"What a sight we are," Tom joked between the tears. "War is not the great adventure I thought it would turn out to be."

We sat in silence. Everything was so quiet you could have sworn there was not a war going on.

A voice cut through the stillness.

"I can't let you alone for a few minutes without you getting in trouble!"

It was Captain O'Sullivan.

"Sorry, captain!" I said, wiping my eyes. "How did you know I was here?"

Seamus and Phelim appeared. They had big grins on their faces.

"I should have known!" I laughed.

The captain untied me.

"What are you doing, sir?" I asked.

"It's all right. I've had a word with the commanding officer."

"The lieutenant?"

"No, the brigadier."

"When you want something, go to the top!" Seamus joked.

"Or you could just steal, the way you normally do!" Phelim countered.

Seamus was indignant. "I have never stolen anything in my life. I may have borrowed certain items which were required at the time, but I have never ever stolen something from someone that didn't deserve it!"

Aoife and Tom helped me up on my feet.

Captain O'Sullivan addressed us all.

"There is something special about this group. I have had approval from my superiors that you can all stick together from now on as one team of stretcher-bearers. You won't have to face the horrors of the battlefield alone."

"Excuse me, sir, does that include Tom?"

"Yes, it does. Now get back to camp the lot of you before you get me in trouble!" the captain joked. "I'll see you all there later."

Tom started to protest as we walked back. "I don't want to be a stretcher-bearer. I want to fight!"

Aoife fixed him with her steely gaze. "You'll do as you are told, Tom Boyle. You should not even be here in the first place!"

"What do you mean?"

"You're only fifteen! You'll stick with us until we get you safely back home. And, while I'm at it, send a letter to your parents to let them know you're all right!"

"That's telling you, Tom!" Seamus laughed.

"Don't mess with John. He knows what's he's talking about!" Phelim warned.

"Fifteen is no big deal," I chimed in, without thinking. "Sure I'm only twelve!"

Tom looked at me in bewilderment. "Twelve?"

Aoife raised her arms in despair. "Never mind him! He acts like a twelve-year old! He's eighteen years old!"

"Are you sure?" Tom probed.

"As sure as my name is John!" Aoife replied.

Phelim and Seamus burst into laughter.

Tom shook his head and smiled. "You are a very strange bunch – has anyone ever told you that?"

Then we all laughed.

Chapter 5

April-May 1915: The Second Battle of Ypres, Belgium, and Captain Adrian Carton de Wiart

The additional medical training we received proved invaluable over the next few months. Without it we would not have been able to help wounded soldiers from both sides during the fighting. By now Aoife and I were so involved in the war we had little or no time to miss our home.

One day Captain O'Sullivan came to see us.

"There's an attack planned near the town of Ypres. Your group is going to provide some medical assistance."

We were transported by truck 40 kilometres north to the town of Ypres in Belgium.

When we arrived at the camp, a captain on horseback appeared. He had just been inspecting the line of troops.

He stopped beside me. I was staring up at him when his chestnut-brown horse turned its head and sniffed me. Then it licked me in the face.

"Ferdia!" I gasped.

"My horse seems to like you!" the captain laughed. "I don't have anyone to take care of him. I know you are stretcher-bearers but perhaps you can help me with him?"

"Glad to, sir," I replied.

"The last person in charge of him wasn't up to the task and got his arm broken when the horse kicked him. Have you ever worked with horses, lad?"

"Yes, sir!" I replied, looking forward to a chance of spending time with Ferdia who had saved me from many dangers in the time of Oliver Cromwell.

"My friends have worked with horses as well, sir!" I said.

"Bring them all! I lost the other stable hands who were good with horses."

"What happened to them, sir?" Seamus asked.

"All blown up by a stray shell. Very unfortunate."

Phelim and Seamus looked at one another with raised eyebrows.

"My name is Captain Adrian Carton de Wiart so you'll be reporting directly to me on any equine matters as well as medical matters.'

"Equine, sir?" Seamus asked.

"*Horses!*" I whispered to him.

Captain de Wiart wore an eye patch. He noticed me looking at it.

"Lost an eye in Somaliland in 1914," he said before I

had a chance to ask. "I was shot twice in the face. I lost part of my ear too – look!" He turned his head to show us his damaged ear.

Seamus looked very impressed.

"Do you know what's going to happen in the next attack, sir?" I asked.

"I can't tell you that, lad, for reasons of security. All I can say is count your blessings that you won't be fighting on the front line in the battle that is to come." He swung Ferdia around and trotted off, calling over his shoulder, *"Report to my headquarters immediately!"*

We set off and when we got there we were shown to the stables.

Ferdia was already there. He bounced around in his stall and whinnied in excitement when he saw us approach.

"Stop that racket, you silly bag of wind! The Germans will hear you!" Phelim warned.

"How far away are they?" I asked.

"A couple of miles at most, possibly closer. It's the snipers you need to watch out for. They'll be looking to climb up any nearby trees and take pot shots at us!"

I picked up a horse brush and started to brush Ferdia's coat. Then we swept out the stables and got some fresh straw.

The next day we had to rise at five along with the captain. He was a very early riser. Ferdia was ready for his inspection.

Captain de Wiart smiled when he saw the horse.

"I've never seen him look so well," he said to me. "I can see that you know your way around horses!"

"Thank you, sir – I had some help!" I said as I pointed towards the others.

The captain nodded. "*A little help is worth a lot of pity! Well done to you all!*"

"Thank you, sir!" we replied.

The captain rode out on Ferdia to inspect the troops. When he returned that evening, we took Ferdia back to the stables and took care of him.

🐴 🐴 🐴

The next day the captain and his second-in-command decided to walk out and check some of the trenches as the Second Battle of Ypres raged.

"Why is this called the *Second* Battle of Ypres?" I asked.

"There was one here already in the early months of the war," the captain replied.

"It can't have gone down well, if we're here again!" Seamus muttered.

The captain looked at Seamus but said nothing.

We arrived at the battleground to see what help we

could give to the wounded. There was constant shelling from both sides.

After a few minutes we could see a cloud of some sort drawing near.

"Is that smoke from the shells?" the captain asked his second-in-command.

"It seems to be making its way towards our trenches," he replied.

"That doesn't look like smoke from an exploding shell," Phelim remarked.

"There's a strange smell in the air too," I said. "It smells like chlorine." I was remembering the smell from my school swimming pool.

"*It's poison gas!*" the captain shouted.

The captain reached into his pocket and took out some gauze and cotton pads. He poured some liquid over them and handed one to each of us.

"Place these over your noses and mouths!" he ordered.

There wasn't enough to go round.

"What will I do?" asked Seamus.

"*Stick your head in that bucket of water!*" I shouted, pointing over to a bucket beside a large gun. "That should protect you!"

Seamus ran over, knelt down and thrust his head in.

Fortunately the gas never reached us, but we could see many men running back in great distress. Some were coughing and struggling to breathe. Others were frothing at the mouth. At first some of the officers tried to block the soldiers who were running away.

"*Get back here, you cowards!*" they roared.

"*Let them through!*" the captain ordered. "*They're running from the poison gas!*"

The captain was very angry about the gas.

"In all my years as a soldier, I have never seen this before. This is abominable! We'll have to get gas masks. I never thought I would live to see the day when people sank so low. What a horrible way to die."

Seamus walked over to us.

"That was a close one, Seamus!" I said.

"Yes, yes, it was. But just to say, the liquid in that bucket was not water!"

"Well, if it wasn't water, what was it?" Aoife asked.

"That's a bucket used to clear the latrine!" Phelim snorted.

"What's a latrine?" Aoife asked.

"It's a toilet dug outside for the soldiers," Tom replied. "Sometimes they use buckets to clear any blockages."

"Let's never speak of this again!" Seamus muttered as he wiped his face with his sleeve.

As we stood there the shells being fired by the German artillery began to land nearer our position.

Captain de Wiart stood upright and refused to duck

down when a shell fell just about a thirty metres away from us.

"Won't you please take cover, sir?" his second-in-command pleaded.

"Certainly not! When my time is up my time is up!" De Wiart stubbornly declared.

Just then we heard a whistling sound.

"It's a shell!" Seamus shouted. *"Run for cover!"*

We dived into a ditch. The captain was thrown to one side by the force of the blast. When we recovered we looked around at the damage caused. We all seemed to be all right.

The captain stood up and shrugged off the blast.

"Where is my second-in-command?" he asked.

We looked around and found a hand on the ground wearing a leather glove.

"That's the kind of glove he likes to wear," the captain observed.

We spread out and searched the area.

"Over here!" Seamus shouted. *"The poor man's body was thrown over here by the force of the explosion!"*

We all ran over.

Phelim tried to console us as we stood over the body. "It was very quick. He felt nothing."

"I hate this war," Tom said.

"We all do," I replied.

The next day we accompanied Captain de Wiart as he

went to inspect his unit. I brought my medical bag with me just in case we encountered any wounded. As we walked along the road we passed by some dead German soldiers lying on the ground.

I said a silent prayer for them as we continued onwards. They were beyond help.

Then a thought struck me.

"Excuse me, captain, but why are we passing German soldiers?"

The captain paused. "You're right! I think we've walked too far! We must have walked into German-held territory! We need to go back!"

Too late! Within seconds we were being fired at. The captain was hit by a bullet and fell to the ground. The firing continued.

Aoife and I found some cover in a trench. Phelim, Seamus and Tom dived to the other side and found some cover behind a wall.

"Are you all right, captain?" I whispered as loudly as I dared – I didn't want the Germans to hear us. "Where are you?"

The captain then jumped in beside us.

"I'm all right! I've just been shot in the hand," he said matter-of-factly.

The hand was covered in blood.

"We'll need to get you patched up, sir," I said.

"Where's our medical bag?" Aoife asked, looking around.

"I dropped it on the road when the shooting started," I said. "Will I go back and get it?"

Aoife shook her head. "No, it's still too dangerous."

"We can use this," the captain suggested as he held up a scarf.

"Where did you get that, sir?" I asked.

"I found it on the road," he replied.

"It must have been worn by one of the soldiers," Aoife said.

We took the scarf and wrapped it tightly around his bloody wrist to lessen the bleeding. It was hard to tell how much of his hand remained – some of it just wasn't there anymore.

When the shooting stopped we all took the captain back to a medical station where he was examined immediately by a doctor.

When he removed the scarf Seamus went very pale. "Look, most of his palm and wrist are completely gone!"

"He's only got two fingers left," said Phelim. "And they're only hanging on by a piece of skin."

The doctor began to treat the hand.

"Pull those two fingers off," Captain de Wiart ordered. "They are of no use to me now."

The doctor disagreed. "I'm not going to do that, sir."

"Oh, don't be so ridiculous! You can't save them. Look, if you won't do it, I'll just have to do it myself!"

There and then, in full view of everyone, he pulled off the two fingers.

Now it was Phelim's turn to turn pale.

Seamus fainted on the spot.

Aoife and I bent down to help him.

"There now, didn't hurt a bit! I say, what's wrong with him?" the captain said when he noticed Seamus lying on the ground.

"He's fine, sir," I said as we managed to get Seamus back up on his feet.

"No Irish person should ever have to see that," Seamus muttered as he tried to steady himself.

The captain's eyes lit up. "Irish, you say? I'm half Irish and half Belgian, you know!"

"Which half is Irish?" Phelim asked as he too struggled to keep on his feet.

"What's that?" the captain asked.

"He's a bit delirious, sir!" I explained.

Now Tom began to grow pale.

"Begging your pardon, sir," he said, "but I think this Irish person is going to be sick!"

I grabbed Tom by the arm. "Come on outside for some air!"

The rest of the night passed without incident. The captain was transferred to another hospital and we were sent back to our old unit.

We soon settled back into a daily routine and were assigned back to Captain O'Sullivan for the next battle to come.

Chapter 6

May 1915: The Battle of Aubers Ridge, France

Seamus came into the camp carrying a newspaper. Aoife was with him.

"Have you heard the news?" he asked as he held up the front page.

We looked at the headline.

"*LUSITANIA* SUNK BY A SUBMARINE, PROBABLY 1,260 DEAD. TWICE TORPEDOED OFF IRISH COAST."

Aoife shook her head. "Those poor people."

Phelim grabbed the newspaper and read the details. "This was a British passenger ship, but it had 128 American passengers. It will bring the Americans into the war, without doubt!"

"They've broken the rules of warfare," Seamus remarked.

"What rules?" Aoife asked.

"The sinking of civilian ships during wartime is just not done. Even the pirates of old would not attack civilian ships ... most of the time."

Phelim continued to read. "The ship was sunk without any warning so the passengers did not have a chance to get to the lifeboats. The boat sank in twenty minutes. There's a quote from Winston Churchill, the Lord of the Admiralty: *'The poor babies who perished in the ocean struck a blow at German power more deadly than could have been achieved by the sacrifice of 100,000 men.'*"

"That's terrible," Aoife said.

"I bet this will be enough to drag America into this war," Seamus said.

"No, it won't," I said firmly. "It's not time for them to join in yet."

"And how do you know this?" Seamus asked.

Then all of us together yelled, *"School project!"*

It was an old joke of ours from the days I had first met Seamus and Phelim in the days of Cromwell, when they had no idea what a 'school project' meant.

Tom arrived back at the camp.

"Why all the glum faces? Have I missed something?"

Phelim showed him the newspaper.

Tom frowned. "Grim news indeed. And I have some more news for you. We are about to be transferred."

"Where are we going?" I asked as we walked

towards the trucks that would transport us.

Tom shrugged his shoulders. "No idea, it's all very hush hush."

Seamus grinned. "Maybe they're bringing us to a luxury hotel!"

Captain O'Sullivan gave us a briefing later that day.

"I have received fresh orders from command. We are going to help the French. They are planning a surprise attack on the Germans."

"Why the hurry all of a sudden? Tom asked.

"Germany is fighting on two fronts at the moment," he replied. "They are fighting us on the Western Front and the Russians on the Eastern Front. They have sent a lot of their soldiers and supplies to the Eastern Front."

"They'll try and defeat Russia quickly so that they can concentrate their attack on the Western Front then," I said, remembering this from Sanjay's notes.

"Exactly. So the French, with support from ourselves, are going to try to launch a surprise attack north of Arras to try and catch them unawares. We'll launch an attack at the same time at Aubers Ridge. Hopefully both we and the French can break through the German line. We need every soldier we can get. I need you five to provide the medical support. There are going to be a lot of wounded people."

On Saturday evening, May 8th, 1915, we stood in our trench, checking our medical equipment.

"I've just heard that there's an Irish unit, the Royal Munster Fusiliers nearby," Seamus suggested. "Let's go over to meet them before the battle tomorrow."

"Good idea. There might not be any of us around tomorrow," Phelim replied.

"There you go again!" Seamus replied. "Always the glass half empty with you. Come on, misery guts!"

"What's a fusilier?" Aoife asked.

Seamus and Phelim looked blankly at Aoife.

"It's a person in the army who is armed with a fusil, which is a light musket, which is a light gun with a long barrel," I said.

"I was just going to say that!" Seamus said.

"Of course you were!" Phelim mocked him. "Just as well there's someone around here with a bit of education!"

We met the Munster Fusiliers near the village of Rue de Bois. They had stopped at a shrine.

"What's going on?" Tom asked one of the soldiers.

"We're getting a blessing from Father Gleeson before the battle tomorrow. See him over there." The soldier pointed to two men in the distance on horses.

"Who is that with him?" I asked.

"That's Lieutenant-Colonel Rickard – he's in charge."

We moved closer to hear the words of Father Gleeson: "*Miseratur vestri omnipotens Deus, et dismissis omnibus peccatis vestris, perducat vos Iesus Christus ad vitam aeternam."*

"What did he say, I wonder?" Seamus asked.

"It's Latin," I replied. "He said 'May Almighty God have mercy on you and, having forgiven all your sins, may Jesus Christ bring you to life everlasting.'"

Seamus looked at me. "Don't tell me that was a 'school project'?"

"No! It's a gift. I can understand lots of languages!" I joked, winking at Aoife.

"Where are you soldiers from?" Aoife asked a group who stood near us.

"Most of us are from Cork and Kerry," one of them replied.

"I wish I was back in Kerry now," another said. "Will you be fighting with us tomorrow then? We're attacking from the south."

"We'll be coming from the north, so we'll see you somewhere in the middle!" Seamus said.

"I hope we all make it!" one of them said.

We all shook hands before we left.

"See you on the other side," one of them said.

Then everyone bowed their heads and sang two hymns – "Te Deum" and "Hail Glorious, St. Patrick".

That night we waited in the trenches for dawn. A combination of nerves and fear meant that nobody was able to sleep.

The sun rose just after four and everything was quiet.

"What a beautiful dawn!" I said.

Aoife agreed. "The sun is in its heaven. Everything is as it should be."

"The calm before the storm," Seamus whispered.

The bombardment started at five o'clock.

Tom looked out.

"They're clearing the way for the attack," he said. "The shelling should destroy some of the barbed wire and land in some of the German trenches."

An explosion near our trench made the ground beneath us shake.

"What was that?" Seamus asked. "Are the German bombs reaching us?"

"No, that was one of ours!" Tom said. "Our own bombs are falling short!"

After about half an hour of constant shelling the order came to go over the top.

We waited, cowering down in the trench while the battle raged.

Aoife and Tom looked scared. I tried to put on a brave face, but I don't think I was very successful. Seamus and Phelim must have seen our fear.

At last the shelling and shooting stopped.

"Stay close to us," Seamus said as we got ready to move out to help the wounded.

"Don't worry, we'll see you all get through this safely," Phelim added.

When it seemed safe to do so, we climbed out and made our way through no man's land. Suddenly the sound of a machine gun rang out. The five of us managed to make our way through a gap in the barbed wire and dived into a hole made by the shells of one of the large guns.

"We can't go any further!" I said. "We'll be cut down."

Seamus agreed. "You're right, lad!" He put his helmet on the end of his rifle and lifted it above the lip of the hole. It was shot at immediately. He pulled it back down. It had two bullet holes in it.

"That could have been my head in that!"

Phelim shook his head. "Don't worry, it never would have hit your pea of a brain!"

Seamus protested. "I'll have you know my brain is as big as an orange!"

At this stage the German shelling began so it was hard to tell which side was firing what shells.

Two soldiers jumped into the same trench we were in. They were Germans!

"*Stop, don't shoot! We surrender!*" they shouted in English, throwing down their guns and lifting their hands in the air.

One of them kept laughing and grinning.

"What's wrong with him?" Tom asked.

"He has what you call *'shell shock'*," the other German soldier replied. "He is no danger to anyone except perhaps himself."

The shells were now starting to fall near our positions. Aoife, Tom and I were now in fear of our lives.

"We can't stay here!" I shouted.

"Well, we can't go forward!" Aoife said. "We'll be cut to pieces."

"We can't go backwards either," Tom said. "Some of our own shells are falling near our positions."

"We need to send someone out to do a reconnaissance and get some orders on what to do next," Phelim suggested.

"The people back at the headquarters behind our own lines need to know what's happening," Tom said. "We're getting slaughtered!"

"Heading back would be dangerous," Phelim warned.

"I'll do it! Danger is my middle name!" Seamus started to get up but Phelim pulled him back down.

"I thought it was Rupert!" he said, laughing.

"I'll do it," I volunteered. "I'm the quickest and I'm a smaller target, so I'll be harder to hit."

Aoife grabbed my arm in a panic.

I gently took her hand and held it. "I'll be all right," I said. "I'll be back soon. Look after Tom. Tom, you look after – eh, John." I managed to stop myself from saying Aoife's name.

"Stop right there, Liam – there's no way you're leaving this hole!" Phelim growled.

I jumped up and out before he could stop me and started to run towards my own lines. The bullets were being fired around me and I looked in vain for a path back to our own trenches. The barrage of fire in front of me was so strong I had to veer sideways away from our own line.

I picked up a rifle that was lying on the ground. I hoped that I would not have to use it. I suddenly realised that I was now closer to the German guns than our own. A lone German soldier ran towards me. I leaped into a ditch to get out of sight. He did not notice me and ran past. He was tall and thin and had a black moustache. He seemed to be holding a leather pouch. He must have been a dispatcher, carrying a message from the front line back to German headquarters.

If I could get the message he was holding, I thought, it might provide some useful information.

I scrambled out of the ditch and ran after him.

"*Stop!*" I shouted.

He kept running. I aimed my rifle at his back and shouted at him again to stop. Still he ran on. If I didn't fire in the next few seconds he would be out of range. Could I do it? Could I take the life of another person? I took a deep breath and put my finger on the trigger.

The sudden whinnying of a horse distracted me. *Ferdia!* He ran towards me from the trees. The soldier looked back at me and the horse for an instant and then disappeared into the distance. The sound of a shell exploding nearby brought me back to my senses. I jumped onto Ferdia's back and held tightly to his mane as he galloped away from the shelling. Soon we were back at the command centre where I reported that our shells were falling short.

I hopped back onto Ferdia and we galloped off towards the danger zone. I stopped him short just as he was about to bring me into no man's land.

"No, Ferdia, you'll get hurt! Let me off here. I'll be all right. Get yourself to safety before anyone sees you!"

Ferdia stood in front of me for a moment. Then, after lifting his head in and the air and snorting, he ran off into the trees.

"See you soon," I whispered.

When the shelling stopped I retraced my steps carefully over no man's land and got back to the crater.

"Anyone down there?" I whispered. "Don't shoot, it's me!"

"Who is me?" asked a voice I recognised as Seamus's.

"That's Liam, you ninny goat!" I heard Phelim reply.

"Jump on in, lad!"

Tom patted me on the back when I got back in. "Well done, Liam! That was a very brave thing to do!"

"Remind me to have a serious chat with you later about obeying your elders!" Phelim warned.

As we got ready to abandon the crater, there was a question about what we were going to do with the German prisoners.

I decided to speak up. "We need to take these prisoners with us. Are you all with me on this?"

Seamus, Aoife and Phelim looked at Tom who nodded in agreement.

"You're right, Liam," he said. "These men have surrendered. It is our duty to treat them accordingly."

As soon as there was a brief lull in the shelling we scrambled out of the crater and began to crawl back towards our own line. Seamus went first, followed by Aoife, myself, the German soldiers, Phelim and Tom. We had to crawl over the bodies of dead soldiers, what was left of them. Many had been blown to pieces by the shelling.

As we crawled by one injured young soldier, he called out in pain.

"Help me, please!"

"He's alive!" Aoife said.

"You all go ahead," I whispered. "I'll stay. Go on now. I'll follow you soon."

"I'm staying too," Aoife insisted.

I did not argue.

We dragged the soldier into a small trench to avoid any further gunfire.

"I'm sorry for stopping you," he gasped. "Save yourselves. There's no hope for me."

"Hush now, don't you be silly. We'll stay as long as we need to," Aoife whispered, stroking his hand.

"That's right," I agreed. "Is there anything we can do for you?"

"I'm so thirsty."

I gave him a drink of water from my flask.

"It tastes like petrol," he said.

"Sorry," I said. "They bring up the water in petrol cans. They don't always get the opportunity to rinse out the petrol before adding the water."

"That's all right. Thank you. I feel better now."

Aoife held his hand.

"What's a girl doing on the battlefield?"

"How do you know I'm a girl?"

"It's funny how clear things become when death is approaching."

"Don't talk like that," Aoife said.

"The last girl I spoke to was my mother, when I said goodbye to her. I've only been here a few weeks, you know. Oh, Mother, I miss you! I'll never hear you sing to me again."

Aoife began to sing quietly:

"It's a long way to Tipperary, it's a long way to go
It's a long way to Tipperary to the sweetest girl I know…"

The young soldier squeezed Aoife's hand.

"Mother!" he gasped and then he was gone.

"He couldn't have been any more than eighteen," Aoife said with tears in her eyes.

"Come on, Aoife, we have to get back. We have to save ourselves."

Aoife put the soldier's helmet over his face. We set off again and caught up with the group who had stayed in another shell hole, waiting for us. As we all struggled to make our way towards our own lines, we thought we were far enough away from the German guns and decided to stand up and make a dash for it. The German soldier who was suffering from shell shock started to run towards the trenches. A voice rang out.

"The Germans are launching a counterattack. Fire! Fire!"

"No! They're prisoners! They're surrendering!" Tom shouted.

Shots rang out. I saw the German soldiers fall. Seamus was hit too and collapsed to the ground. I ran in front of Tom to protect him from the gunfire. I felt a sharp pain in my shoulder. As I fell my head hit a rock and everything went black.

I woke up later in a field hospital. My shoulder and head were heavily bandaged.

Two worried faces looked down at me.

It was Aoife and Tom.

"How do you feel?" Aoife asked.

I tried to sit up. "I'm not sure." As I tried to move, I felt a pain in my shoulder and my head throbbed.

"Don't try to sit up – you need to rest," Tom insisted.

"The bullet went clean through your shoulder without hitting a bone," Aoife said. "You're very lucky. You hit your head as you fell so you have concussion."

I rubbed my head and remembered the incident at the Cromwell site in Drogheda where I had hit my head trying to get away from the loose cannon.

"Concussion? Another one?"

"Just as well you've a thick head!" she said, laughing.

"You saved my life!" Tom said. "That bullet was meant for me!"

"How long have I been here?"

"Three days."

"What about Seamus?"

"I'm here, in the bed next to you!"

And so he was.

"He's okay," Aoife said. "He got shot in the head."

"Fortunately, the bullet went straight through without hitting any vital organs, like his brain – but then his brain is the size of an orange so that's no surprise!"

Phelim joked as he arrived.

Seamus sat up. "Steady on, it's a very big orange! More like a grapefruit! No, more like a melon! That's how big it is! The size of a melon!"

"It's a miracle you can squeeze it into that head of yours!" Phelim retorted.

Aoife smiled. "The bullet grazed his forehead," she told me, "so he'll be all right."

"What about the two German soldiers?" I asked.

"They didn't make it, lad," Seamus said. "The soldiers panicked and fired on them. The Brigadier General tried to intervene and impose some kind of order, but he was killed too, possibly by his own soldiers!"

"How bad was it in the battle?" I asked.

"Over 11,000 dead," Tom said. "Most of them were killed close to their own trenches. They barely made it out of them."

"What about our unit – the Royal Irish Rifles?"

"467 dead."

The tears began to well up in my eyes. "Where is Captain O'Sullivan?"

"Amos didn't make it …"

We all fell silent.

"What about the Munster Fusiliers?"

Tom looked to the ground. "398 dead …"

Aoife shook her head. "Those poor lads."

Phelim sighed. "They haven't been able to find all of the bodies."

Aoife intervened. "Phelim, I think that's enough for the moment. Liam needs to sleep."

"No, I want to know. Why can't they find the bodies?"

"They may have been completely destroyed by the shells or got swallowed up in the mud."

"Don't mention mud to me," Phelim said. "The more rain that falls the muddier the trenches get. As you walk along the trench the mud gets sloppier, wetter and deeper."

"What was the point of all of this? Was it worth it?" Tom asked.

"It's hard to make sense of it," Seamus replied. "The Germans are claiming victory – and there are complaints that the shells and ammunition on our side were faulty."

I shook my head. "All of those lives . . ."

Over the next few weeks Seamus and I recovered our strength. Seamus was discharged first from the hospital. I was able to leave a few weeks later.

As I was leaving the hospital I passed a number of nurses huddled in a corner, crying.

"Is everything all right?" I asked.

"They shot her!" one of the nurses sobbed. "Can you believe it? They shot her!"

"Who shot who?" I asked

"Nurse Edith Cavell. She was shot by the Germans for helping British soldiers to escape from Belgium! How could they be so horrible?"

I touched the cheek which had been kissed so long ago by this brave lady and left the hospital in a daze. I could not think straight. How had it come to this? Who would shoot a nurse?

The next few weeks passed by in a blur. I didn't say much to anyone. I kept very much to myself.

Phelim thought a change of scene might help, so Aoife and I were assigned temporarily to help out in the army kitchens.

Before we knew it, the year 1916 was upon us.

♞ ♞ ♞

"Hello there, youngsters! Is there anything to eat?" Seamus asked one day as he came back from his sentry duties.

"You're always thinking of food!" I laughed.

"Only when I'm not eating!" he replied.

"What are you doing here anyway?" Aoife asked as she ladled a portion of stew for him from a large pot.

"I'm here to fetch yourself and Liam. We're all being moved back to the front line. There's going to be a big push in 1916 to end the war. We're needed to help train the new recruits. There's thousands of them and most of them have never held a gun in their lives!"

"Where have all of these extra troops come from?" Aoife asked. "I thought joining the army was voluntary?"

"They've just gone and introduced conscription in Britain. Any single man or widower without children, aged between eighteen and forty-one, is expected to apply to join the fighting. We're expecting a couple of hundred any day now."

"What about Ireland?"

"No conscription there," he replied. "The British know it would be opposed."

"How are we expected to train these new recruits?" I asked.

"We're just training the medical personnel. We'll try and show them how to stay alive and save lives. That's all we can do really."

"Are the others all right?"

"Oh yes, Tom and Phelim will be helping with the training too."

Chapter 7

April 1916: The Easter Rising, Ireland

Over the next few months as we trained the new recruits, news came through about the Easter Rising in Ireland. Members of the Irish Republican Brotherhood and the Irish Citizens Army, led by Pádraig Pearse and James Connolly, took over different parts of Dublin in a rebellion against British rule. After six days the Irish surrendered. Hundreds were killed and over a thousand were injured. Dublin city centre was badly damaged after being bombed and all of the leaders were arrested.

"What a bunch of cowards! Stabbing us in the back while we are over here fighting in the British Army!" Tom remarked when he read the newspaper article about the rising.

"They'll probably jail the leaders and it will all be

forgotten in a couple of weeks," Seamus replied. "That's what usually happens."

Within days further news began to filter through about the executions of fourteen of the leaders.

Phelim read out the list: "Pádraig Pearse, Thomas Clarke, Thomas MacDonagh, Joseph Plunkett, Edward Daly, Michael O'Hanrahan, Willie Pearse, John MacBride, Eamonn Ceannt, Michael Mallin, Seán Hueston, Con Colbert, Thomas Kent, Seán Mac Diarmada and James Connolly. All shot by firing squad."

Seamus shook his head. "They say Connolly would have been dead in a few days anyway. He had been shot in the leg and had developed a gangrene infection that would have killed him."

"They didn't have to execute them," Tom said, as his attitude changed. "The Irish people won't easily accept this."

"They might not have supported the rebels in the beginning, but they'll change their mind now," I said. "Home Rule will never be enough now. *'All changed, changed utterly, a terrible beauty is born.'*"

"Where did you hear that?" Tom asked.

"From William Butler Yeats, the poet."

"When did he write that?"

"He hasn't written it yet, but he will, very soon."

Aoife darted a look at me and shook her head.

Tom looked mystified.

Seamus laughed. "Liam can be a barrel of information, Tommy boy – trust him, he's usually right!"

"Look at them," Seamus observed one morning as we were putting some new recruits through their paces.

"What's wrong with them?" I asked

"They're way too cheerful."

"You'd think they're going to a football match or a holiday," Phelim agreed.

"Well, there's a first!" I laughed.

"What's that?" Phelim asked.

"You and Seamus in agreement!"

They looked at one another and then at me.

Phelim growled. "Don't get too used to it!"

"They do look cheerful," I said. "How many of them will survive, I wonder?"

"Best not to think too much about it," Phelim said.

Despite our warnings, some of the new recruits made basic mistakes which got them killed. One young soldier lit a cigarette during the night and was an easy target for a German sniper. Another stood up in a trench to investigate a noise he had heard. He thought it was a cat in trouble. The poor chap was killed as soon as he showed his head. It turned out that it wasn't a cat. It was a large rat which continued to walk through the area without harm. Rats were a huge problem in the trenches. They were everywhere. Many of them were the size of a small dog.

"How are they so big?" Aoife asked.

"It's all the dead bodies – every night there's a feast lying in wait for them," Phelim answered sadly.

One night I was sleeping and I felt something furry trying to burrow into the sleeve of my coat. It was a rat! I jumped up in fright and it fell to the ground. I aimed a kick at it but missed and it ran off into the darkness.

I screamed. Aoife screamed. Tom screamed!

"What are you screaming for! It's only a little rat!" Seamus laughed as he reached for his food tin.

When he opened it he found a rat inside eating what was left of his biscuits.

"Right, that's it!" he roared. *"I'm declaring all-out war on these rats! I can put up with a lot of things, but a person's biscuits are sacred!"*

Phelim looked at him suspiciously. "I didn't know you had biscuits! Where did you get them?"

"Never mind that now, we need to get rid of this infestation!" Seamus roared. *"Operation Ratcatcher is now formally in session!"*

We spent the night tracking down the rats in our trenches by leaving trails of crumbs in certain areas for them to follow. It didn't take long for them to appear.

Seamus got ready to hit one over the head with a shovel.

"Don't kill them!" Aoife pleaded.

"Well, how else are we going to get rid of them?" Tom asked. "They ate my biscuits as well!"

"Please!" Aoife begged. "They're creatures too!"

"All right then," Seamus sighed.

So we spent the night trapping them in makeshift traps and throwing them over the trench into no man's land where they scurried off into the darkness.

We caught eighty-three of them that night.

"They'll be back tomorrow," Seamus warned.

"If they come back, we'll catch them again," Aoife replied, "and get rid of them humanely!"

And that's what we did, every night after that.

"This makes no sense," Seamus said one night after we had finished our latest round of evictions. "Thousands and thousands of soldiers are being killed every day and here we are saving a bunch of rats!"

"All life is precious, Seamus," Aoife replied.

Tom spoke up. "Well said, John. If we had more generals and leaders like you, then perhaps all of this killing and this war itself might have been avoided."

Phelim scratched his stubbly chin. "You may have a point there, Tommy boy!"

Chapter 8

July-November 1916: The Battle of the Somme, France

It wasn't long before we bumped into Captain de Wiart once again. This time he was walking with the aid of a walking stick.

"Well, well, aren't you chaps a sight for sore eyes!" he said.

"How are you, sir? How is the hand?" I asked.

He held up his arm. The hand was completely gone. Only a stump remained.

"I had it removed completely. It wasn't getting any better and the surgeons were just cutting bit after bit off it. It was completely useless!"

"Did it hurt?" Aoife asked.

"Just like going to the dentist!"

Phelim shook his head. "Remind me never to go to *his* dentist!" he whispered in my ear.

"What do you miss most, the hand or the eye?" Seamus asked.

We all looked at Seamus.

"Well, I was just wondering!"

The captain grinned. "Excellent question! In India, they have a saying: '*The one-eyed person sees everything.*' But I miss the eye more than the hand. I use my teeth to help me tie my laces or a necktie. However, I can only see well from one side, so that can be quite frustrating."

"Are you still in the cavalry, sir?" Tom asked.

"No, I've moved to the infantry. We're getting ready for the big battle in the Somme."

"We?"

He introduced us to a man standing dutifully behind him.

"Yes, this man here is my servant, Holmes. He provides wonderful service, don't you, Holmes!"

"Indeed, sir," Holmes replied, bowing slightly.

"Why is he carrying a blanket and small stove, sir?" I queried.

"The two most important elements required in war – warmth and decent food. I don't let Holmes carry a weapon. He fired a rifle near my ear once and I swore he'd never do it again! I don't carry a weapon either, just my walking stick!"

Holmes bowed his head again and agreed. "Very wise, sir, very wise."

"I say, Holmes, while I think of it, that soup you left me this morning didn't taste the best."

"Soup, sir?"

"Yes, the brown soup you left in the cup for me."

"That wasn't soup, sir, that was hot water for shaving. It was the cleanest water I could find. I heated it for you."

The captain cleared his throat and quickly changed the subject.

"What date is it today, Holmes?"

"The 30th day of June, sir."

"The battle is due to start tomorrow!" the captain whispered. "It is going to be one of the biggest bombardments ever from the British. They say the battle should be over in five days!"

Seamus threw his eyes up to heaven. "Where have I heard that before?"

"What do you mean?" De Wiart asked.

"The war was supposed to be over by Christmas 1914!"

The captain nodded. "Well, yes, I suppose you have a point there. I think the powers that be may indeed be overly optimistic. I don't think we have enough guns, particularly as General Haig wants different areas attacked at the same time."

"Does that mean the guns will have to cover a very large area?" I asked.

"Quite so! Why do you ask?"

"Well, if they have to cover a large area they may not be as effective," I replied.

As we stood in the trenches the next day waiting for the fighting to begin, Captain de Wiart addressed the troops.

"There'll be plenty of mud, blood and killing here. I hope you're all ready for it!"

We were based at La Boisselle which was a German stronghold. As we looked out from the trenches we could see the bodies of dead soldiers lying in no man's land ahead of us.

The order came for our soldiers to go over the top and attack.

Captain de Wiart used his teeth to pull the pins out of hand grenades. He then used his good arm to throw them at the opposing army. As usual, we followed behind the troops to help with the injured.

The attack was successful and we were able to reach the German trenches. But the loss of life was horrific. The area of La Boiselle was completely destroyed.

After resting for a while, we were then sent to take part in an attack on High Wood which was being shelled heavily by the Germans.

We met De Wiart again on the battlefield with his servant Holmes. He was taking shelter in a shell hole. He was in low spirits.

"I have lost another of my officers. There are not many of them left now. After all we have been through together. It gets harder and harder to lose people who you know and like."

Holmes handed him a cup of dark liquid.

"I don't feel like shaving at the moment, Holmes."

"Oh no, sir, you can drink this. It's a tot of rum."

We climbed out of the hole and walked along in the dark. The guns were still firing around us.

De Wiart suddenly collapsed onto the ground. We helped Holmes to drag him into a shell hole away from the danger. De Wiart touched the back of his head with his hand. We could see blood.

"Don't touch it, sir, let me look," I suggested.

Holmes and Seamus helped me to roll him over. I could see that he had been shot in the back of the head. Aoife and I applied some dressing to help stop the bleeding. He remained conscious for the next couple of hours.

"Surely his luck has run out now," Phelim whispered to me. "He can't get through this."

"Keep talking," Aoife suggested. "We need to keep you awake, sir, so that you do not lose consciousness."

"Quite right, quite right," the captain replied unsteadily.

"Well now, what should we talk about?" Holmes asked.

"What's more effective, a bullet or a shell?" Seamus asked.

"Well, a shell is definitely more destructive," Holmes replied.

"True," Seamus replied, "but it destroys the area it hits."

"Indeed, then you can't use the buildings or facilities," Holmes agreed.

Tom chipped in. "A bullet is effective for precise killing. One shot in the right area and bang! You're gone. No harm to buildings, roads or countryside."

We all looked at Tom in surprise.

"Well, I'm just saying, that's all!"

"Oh, how my missus would laugh if she could see me now!" Holmes remarked.

"I'm not quite sure she'd be laughing, Holmes," De Wiart said weakly.

We continued talking for a few hours until eventually the shelling stopped.

Then we carried Captain de Wiart back to a dressing station where he was examined by a doctor.

The doctor scratched his head. "Well, you've been shot in the head, no doubt about it, but I can't tell if your skull has a fracture or not. Do you feel any pain?"

"No, not at all, doctor."

The doctor continued the examination. "It appears the bullet that hit you has gone straight through the back of your head without damaging any vital organs. It's quite incredible."

"His brain must be even smaller than yours!" Phelim whispered to Seamus.

The doctor finished his examination. "You've been very lucky, captain."

Seamus looked on in disbelief.

"Lucky? The man has lost an eye, a hand and has now been shot in the head."

De Wiart laughed. "Yes, but I'm still alive! Oh no, Holmes! Where is it?"

"What is it, sir?" Holmes replied in alarm.

The captain looked around frantically. "My walking stick? Have you seen it?"

"No, sir, it must have been left when you were shot!"

The captain was crestfallen. "Oh, dash it, I really liked that stick!"

"It looks like you might be the soldier that cannot be killed, sir!" I joked, trying to take his mind off his loss.

"Well, Liam, I'm not so sure about that! It just is not my time yet. Doctor, have you heard any news on the battle?"

The doctor looked at us sadly. "Not good, I'm afraid. Lots of casualties. Eight officers who had just been assigned to the 8th Battalion this afternoon have been killed already."

"But that's my battalion!"

"I'm sorry, sir. Now, with your injuries, we'll have to get you back to a hospital in England for a thorough check-up. They have better facilities there."

As we saw him off in an ambulance, Phelim said to me "There's no way we'll see him again after that. He can't recover from that!"

Even I had my doubts about his recovery.

The Battle of the Somme did not end until November that year, four months after it began.

"So much for a five-day battle!" Seamus said. "I told them it would last longer. Here we are almost at the end of 1916 and this war just keeps going on and on!"

"They say the British and French armies have lost about 600,000 men in this battle alone," Phelim said.

"Yes, and the Germans have lost almost 500,000," I added.

"How can they all accept such loss of life so easily?" Aoife asked.

Seamus shook his head. "Don't look for common sense during wartime. You won't find it."

"What's this thing called the Hindenburg Line I hear the officers talking about?" Tom asked.

"I think I can answer that one," I replied. "The new leader of the German army is General Hindenburg. He has decided that the Germans should withdraw so that they can adopt a more defensive position in northern

France. They're calling this defensive position the Hindenburg Line."

"How do you know all of this?" Tom asked in disbelief.

"From something called a school project," Seamus chipped in. "I must get one of them whatever they are!"

Phelim shook his head. "Can you believe it? Their German comrades fought and died in battle to keep these areas. Now they are just moving out and handing everything over without a bullet being fired."

"There's still plenty of life in this war yet, God help us!" Seamus said.

We were sleeping on our bunks some time later when Seamus came running in to wake us.

"The Americans have declared war on Germany!" he shouted.

"Well, it's about time. It took them three years to do it!" Phelim replied.

"Why did they decide to get involved now? Was it the U-boats sinking American ships that did it?" Tom asked.

Phelim shook his head. "No, it was all because of a telegram!"

We all looked confused.

"A telegram?" Aoife asked.

"Yes, the Germans sent a telegram to Mexico that said if Mexico supported Germany in a war against the USA,

Germany would give it Texas, Arizona and New Mexico!"

"How very generous of them!" Seamus said sarcastically.

"Everything will change now," I remarked. "The extra American soldiers will tip the balance into finally putting an end to all of this."

I was right of course, but it took a little longer than I remembered.

Chapter 9

July-November 1917: The Third Battle of Ypres, Belgium, and the poet Francis Ledwidge

It took a few months before American soldiers reached Europe, and in the meantime we had to prepare for another battle at Ypres, where we met our old friends Captain de Wiart and Holmes again.

"That fella has more lives than a cat!" Phelim remarked.

"It's Holmes I'd be more worried about!" Seamus replied.

"Why do you say that?"

"Have you not noticed, it's the people around the captain that seem to die, while he seems to get through whatever is thrown at him!"

De Wiart saw us and came over to say hello.

Seamus started to move away. "I'm not standing beside him!"

We were met with a friendly greeting. "Well, well, we meet again!"

"Good to see you looking well, sir, and with another walking stick!" I remarked seeing him holding one.

"It's the actual stick I lost when I was shot! Yes, I walked back to the area a few weeks later when I had recovered and there it was lying in the grass! Lucky, what?"

"Very lucky, sir!" I agreed.

Seamus continued to keep his distance. Phelim also started to edge away from us. Tom followed him too. Aoife looked on and threw her eyes up to heaven.

When the battle began, we were soon caught up in the thick of it, helping the wounded.

"They're calling this the Third Battle of Ypres," Phelim remarked.

"They say good things happen in threes, don't they?" Seamus replied.

"Not this time," Tom said.

Holmes appeared later in the day during one of the attacks. He was very upset.

"Are you all right, Mr. Holmes?" I asked.

Holmes bit his lip and started to shake his head.

"I've lost the captain's blanket and the stove. A shell exploded near me – there was nothing I could do. They were completely destroyed."

I tried to console him. "There, there, Mr. Holmes. I'm sure the captain will understand."

"Do you think so? He liked his blanket and stove. I'm not sure how I'm going to tell him."

"Liam's right," Aoife said. "You're all right. That's what's important. Things can always be replaced. People cannot."

"Tell that to the blooming generals who are sending all the soldiers out into this carnage!" Seamus muttered.

We were soon asked to move to another location to provide assistance. We had to travel along a road that had been badly damaged by shelling and was being repaired by some soldiers.

A dark-haired soldier with a moustache stopped us.

"Are my ears deceiving me? Is that an Irish accent I hear?"

"It is indeed," I said. "I'm Liam O'Malley and this is Seamus, Phelim, Tom and – um, John."

"Where are you from, Liam?"

"Dublin."

"Dublin eh? The Big Smoke! I'm a Meath man myself. Glad to meet you all. My name is Francis Ledwidge."

My eyes bulged. "Francis Ledwidge? The poet?"

The soldier looked surprised. "I didn't think I was that well known! Have you heard of me?"

"Well, of course I have. I have relatives in Meath and Drogheda who know your works very well. I saw some of your poems in the *Drogheda Independent* when my class did a project on your poetry a few weeks ago!"

Seamus nudged Phelim. "There you go, another school project!"

"The *Drogheda Independent* was always good to me," Ledwidge continued. "That newspaper and my sponsor Lord Dunsany helped me to get my poetry to a wider audience. A book of poetry is better than food and warmth, you know."

Just then Seamus's stomach rumbled with hunger.

"Tell that to Seamus!" Aoife said, laughing.

Seamus was indignant. "An empty sack won't stand, you know!"

"Here, have a carrot!" Ledwidge said, taking a carrot from his pocket and handing it over to Seamus. "We got them in a nearby field."

Seamus polished it off before anyone else could have a bite.

"How has it been going, Mr. Ledwidge?" I asked.

"It's not the same since the Easter Rising," he confided. "I don't quite know what the Irish are fighting for any more. My good friend Thomas McDonagh was executed by the British after the Rising. We're over here fighting for them and they killed our own Irish people. How can we ever trust their words again? Poor Thomas!" Then he closed his eyes and spoke a piece of poetry about his lost friend which I knew from my class project.

*"He shall not hear the bittern cry
In the wild sky where he is lain
Nor voices of the sweeter birds
Above the wailing of the rain."*

"Beautiful words," Aoife said.

"I'll never forget how they treated the prisoners after the Rising – for shame, for shame!" Ledwidge continued. "And there I was wearing a British uniform of the Royal Inniskilling Fusiliers, fighting for Home Rule for Ireland! I'll tell you now, there were times that if someone told me the Germans were coming over the back wall I wouldn't have tried to stop them! Then they went and hanged Roger Casement last August in London."

"What was his crime?" Tom asked.

"He tried to smuggle in guns for the Irish rebels to use during the Easter Rising, but he was caught," I replied.

"They hung him like a dog! What a terrible end!" Ledwidge said.

"What are you doing here?" I asked.

"They're keeping me and these five fellows working on repairing the roads for the moment. Some of us are being held in reserve and heading towards the village of Boezinghe."

"Keep your wits about you around here," Phelim warned. "This is the kind of place where German shells could land at any moment without warning."

"Sure don't I know it!" he replied. "I took Holy

Communion from our chaplain Father Devas this morning and we were talking about whether either of us would be there the following day, such is this godforsaken war! I can think of better ways to be spending the last day of July 1917! All our leave has been cancelled because of the upcoming battle. Perhaps we'll be able to go home soon. I can't wait to see my wonderful mother again and to walk by the River Boyne and see Slane one more time."

"There's no place like home!" I agreed, looking at Aoife.

"We're just about to sit down for some tea if you would like to join us?" Ledwidge said.

Seamus's eyes lit up. "Any more carrots?"

"I think we can rustle up something!" Ledwidge laughed as he went to fetch the food.

Just as we were about to sit down, the hooves of a horse could be heard.

It was Ferdia.

Ledwidge came back with the carrots and watched the horse approach in wonder. "Well, would you look at that! Where did that horse appear from?"

"Trust that old nag to turn up once there are a few carrots going!" Phelim muttered just as Seamus grabbed them all and stuffed them into his pockets.

This time however it was not the food Ferdia was after. He raced up to us and stopped beside me. He was in a very agitated state and continually pushed his nose up against my shoulder, trying to move me away from where I was standing.

"What is that silly creature doing?" Seamus asked.

"Perhaps he wants a carrot?" Ledwidge suggested. "I'll get some more."

"I'll come with you," Tom said and walked away with him.

The penny suddenly dropped with Aoife.

"Liam, get up on Ferdia's back!"

"Why?"

"Something's not right. I think Ferdia senses danger!"

"Aoife might be right, lad. Get on the horse!" Seamus roared. *"You too, Aoife!"*

Seamus grabbed me and whooshed me up onto the horse's back. He swung Aoife on too.

"Get back over here, Tom!" he roared.

"What about the rest of you?" I asked.

"Don't worry about us. We'll be following you! *Now go!*" Phelim slapped Ferdia on his hindquarters and he took off at great speed, just as Tom arrived back.

Phelim and the others ran behind us.

"What's the hurry, lads?" Ledwidge shouted as he came back with more carrots.

As Ferdia galloped away we held on as tightly as we could. I held onto his mane. Aoife had her arms around my waist.

Suddenly there was a huge explosion behind us.

"Keep going, Ferdia!" Phelim shouted behind us.

"That was very close!" Aoife shouted.

We kept moving for another few hundred metres until it went completely quiet.

Ferdia slowed down and finally came to a stop. We hopped off. Tom caught up with us.

"It's as if the horse knew there was going to be an explosion!" Tom gasped, breathing heavily.

Phelim and Seamus arrived too and stood bent over, hands on hips, breathing heavily.

"That was a close one!" Seamus gasped.

"Ledwidge and his men!" I cried. "We have to go back and make sure they're all right!"

"Stop, Liam, it might not be safe!" Aoife warned but I was off and running and nobody was going to stop me.

I raced back to the area where we had first met. I arrived first, closely followed by Tom and the others. There was no sign of any of them, only a huge crater in the ground. I fell to my knees in despair and gazed blankly at the large hole in front of me where the poet Francis Ledwidge and his colleagues had stood only minutes previously.

Word soon went around about the explosion and the deaths of the men.

The chaplain Father Devas arrived on the scene and shook his head sadly. He said a prayer as we all bowed our heads.

"Poor Ledwidge, blown to bits," the priest whispered.

"They never had a chance," Tom said.

Aoife and I moved off to where Ferdia stood waiting. He nuzzled us and I knew he was trying to comfort us.

"I'm so sorry, Liam," Aoife said.

"Ferdia knew this was going to happen, didn't he?"

"Yes, he knew somehow."

Seamus and Phelim joined us, for once looking dejected.

"But why didn't Ferdia do something to save Mr. Ledwidge and his friends?"

"Liam – remember we cannot do anything to change what has already happened. These events are already set in time."

"Then what's the point if we can't change anything that has happened?" I shouted.

"Steady on now, lad," said Seamus. "Aoife and Ferdia have your best interests at heart. You know that."

"What do you know about it?" I shouted as tears began to form. "And what precisely is your role here? How come I met you in 1649 during Cromwell's time in Ireland and you and Phelim both just happen to show up during the First World War?"

Phelim didn't answer, instead he arched his eyebrows. *"First* World War? Are you saying there's a *Second* World War after this one?"

"It's best you don't know," Aoife interjected.

"*What?* How stupid can people be?" Seamus said.

Tom came hurrying over. "What's all this going on? I feel I'm missing something! What are you talking about?"

"Liam's upset at the death of Mr. Ledwidge," Phelim said.

Tom put his arm on my shoulder. "Sorry, Liam."

"I want to go home," I sighed.

"We all do, Liam, we all do," said Tom.

I stood up and collected myself. "Come on, let's go. We can't help anyone here."

"Do you want to ride Ferdia for a bit?" Aoife suggested.

"No, thanks, not at the moment," I replied.

Phelim led Ferdia away into the trees and came back without him.

"He'll be fine," Phelim said. "He'll turn up when we need him again."

"What kind of horse is this that goes off on its own and turns up when needed?" Tom asked.

"A special horse!" Aoife replied.

Tom looked more confused than ever.

Seamus put a reassuring arm around him. "Don't think too much about it, lad. Here, fancy a carrot?"

As they went ahead, I walked slowly alongside Aoife with my head down.

"Sorry, Aoife, for shouting at you. I know you're right," I said as we walked along.

"That's all right, Liam – we'll get through this together."

Seamus turned around and waited for us to catch up.

"Does someone need a hug?" Seamus joked on seeing my miserable face.

"Make sure he washes his hands first before you let him near you!" Phelim said.

Seamus was not impressed. "Why don't you wash your mouth out first?"

♞ ♞ ♞

The Third Battle of Ypres started that same day.

"I wonder will they wait for the American troops to arrive before starting any more major battles?" Tom asked.

"Good question," Seamus answered sarcastically. "Let's ask the generals that question when we see them!"

We never did get to ask the generals as we soon encountered more fighting. We did our best to help the casualties on the field but moving forward was a very slow process. Heavy rain made conditions difficult. The heavy shelling destroyed the drainage system on the battlefield so it was soon a battle against water and mud as well as a battle against the Germans. Even the tanks found it hard to move. Trenches were not safe. They could collapse at any moment and men could drown in the mud.

"The order has come from General Plumer to *'bite and hold'*," Phelim told us after a tough day in the trenches.

"What does that mean?" Tom asked.

"Advance a short distance, hold the position, and kill as many of the enemy as they can," Phelim sighed.

♞ ♞ ♞

The battle continued over the next few months.

Everyone was exhausted and morale began to fall within the troops. Any gains made were soon lost through German counterattacks.

Finally, in November, the attacks were ended after the capture of a village called Passchendaele, a town 16 kilometres north of Ypres.

"Such devastation, and for what?" Seamus asked as the five of us were driven away for some rest and relief.

"No general with any intelligence can defend what has taken place over the last few months. It has been a disaster and you can quote me on that!" Phelim said as we left the area.

Eventually, American troops began to arrive. Then news came from the Eastern Front where Russia was engaged in battle with Germany and the Austro-Hungarian Empire, that the hostilities had ceased.

"Russia has signed an armistice with Germany. They are out of the war!" Seamus announced. "It's the Russian Revolution. The Russian Tsar is gone and the Bolsheviks who are now in charge promised to take Russia out of the war. The Russians have surrendered Poland and the Ukraine as well."

Phelim grimaced. "That's bad news. It means the Germans can send most of their troops to the Western Front now. This could add even more years to the war!"

Chapter 10

1918: The War Ends

Phelim was half right. The Germans launched a huge attack in March 1918. At one stage it looked as if they would succeed. However, the Allied Powers, now helped by the Americans, fought back. By July we were told the German army had lost 800,000 soldiers. The end was in sight.

Conditions for the civilian populations were extremely difficult.

"The only people doing well out of this war are the industries making the weapons!" Seamus grumbled.

"There's always money to be made from misfortune," Phelim replied.

"If that was the case then you should be a millionaire," Seamus shot back, "because you are one long string of misery!"

Aoife intervened. "That's enough! It's not getting easier for the civilians either. There is rationing in some countries now. The Germans are so short of food they have been forced to eat turnips that they used to feed to their animals."

"Yeah, well, they started this all off in the first place, so I don't feel too much sympathy," Tom said.

"Where's your compassion?" Aoife asked. "Everyone is suffering!"

"There are food riots as well in some places. The newspapers say there are children and elderly people starving in Germany and Austria," Phelim said.

"What are the leaders doing about it?" I asked.

"They say the army must eat – it doesn't matter if a few old people die or not," Phelim replied.

"It's always the innocent people that suffer the most," Aoife replied. "People have to wear clothes made of woven paper and wooden shoes. There's not enough water and fuel to go around either. There is widespread disease, particularly in the poorer areas. Some people in hospitals are starving to death."

Our unit was now moved to Amiens in France, about 150 kilometres north of Paris and 85 kilometres west of Saint-Quentin, the town where we had started off in the first place.

"The Allies are really going on the attack now!" Seamus announced.

"They've got the Australians and Canadians helping out too," Tom said. "I don't think the war is going to last much longer."

He was right. Large numbers of German soldiers started to surrender. All of their efforts since the start of the year had led to nothing. They were now exhausted and hungry.

Bulgaria, an ally of Germany, surrendered at the end of September. By the middle of October we were informed that most of France and parts of Belgium had been freed of German occupation. We heard word that Germany had contacted the American president Woodrow Wilson with a proposal for an armistice. It was rejected. Turkey surrendered at the end of October thanks to the efforts of the largely Indian army commanded by General Allenby.

As we tended to German prisoners of war who had been wounded, they seemed to have accepted their fate.

One of their artillerymen summed it up. "We know the war is over. How we have looked forward to this moment! Here we are now, humbled, our souls torn and bleeding. We know that we've surrendered."

The head of the army, Ludendorff, resigned and Austria-Hungry, Germany's last ally, surrendered on 4th November.

Parts of the German Army began to refuse to carry out certain attacks which they believed were suicide missions. The end was near.

On the evening of 7th November we were near Haudroy, a place about 60 kilometres east of Saint-Quentin, when there was a bugle call. Everyone feared an attack when suddenly a number of cars with German insignia appeared out of the fog.

A man got out of one of the cars and started to speak.

"My name if Matthias Erzberger. I am here to discuss a possible armistice."

I approached him and in German offered to accompany his group on a trip to a wooded area near Paris where the Allied Powers, under French Marshal Foch, were stationed.

He accepted, I got into the car and we drove out.

When we arrived, I led him and his delegation in to meet Marshal Foch.

"You will act as my interpreter," Marshal Foch ordered when everyone was seated.

"Yes, sir," I replied, going to stand beside his chair.

"Now, I would like you to ask these people what they want."

I translated the request into German. The delegation seemed surprised at the question as they thought their intent was obvious. They took a few moments to respond.

I duly translated Erzberger's reply into French for the Marshal.

"Sir, they have been sent here to discuss armistice terms."

Marshal Foch frowned and beckoned to me to lean down. "I tell you this," he confided, "no matter what happens today, it is my intention to pursue these German soldiers with a sword at their backs to the last minute!"

"Yes, sir," I replied.

He straightened up. "You may now speak to these gentlemen. Tell them that I have no proposals to make. However, I have a list of demands which must be met. Germany will admit it is completely to blame for the war. It will leave any occupied territory in Belgium, Luxembourg and France, including Alsace-Lorraine which they have held since 1870. Allied forces will occupy parts of Germany. Germany will also surrender some of its army resources, such as ships, planes and ammunition. We will blockade German ports and take 5,000 locomotives, 150,000 railway cars and 5,000 trucks."

Herr Erzberger protested when he heard the terms of surrender.

"But, Marshal, the German people are starving. How will we get food to them?"

The Marshal remained unimpressed by his pleas and continued: "As Germany is completely to blame for the war, it will also pay reparations for the war and the destruction it has caused. You have three days to comply."

I translated the message back to the German delegation.

"In the name of God," Herr Erzberger begged, "please do not wait for seventy-two hours. Stop the fighting today!"

Marshal Foch waved away the protests. "You are in no position to dictate terms!"

♘ ♘ ♘

While this was taking place, other events in Germany further hastened the end of the war. Protests were carried out against the Kaiser Wilhelm II, the Emperor of Germany. A general strike broke out in Berlin on November 9th. On that same day the Kaiser abdicated and fled to the Netherlands.

The negotiations to end the war continued. Everything was agreed and signed. The armistice would come into effect at 11a.m. on 11th November 1918 – *"The eleventh hour of the eleventh day of the eleventh month."*

♘ ♘ ♘

"We'll be getting the order to move out one last time very soon," Phelim said as I arrived back in the early hours of the morning of the 11th November.

Seamus agreed. "It will all be over in a few hours. No point in getting people needlessly killed. So let's keep out of harm's way until 11 a.m. this morning."

Phelim nodded. "That's the most sensible thing you've said today."

"Well, the day is still young!" Seamus quipped. "Who in their right mind is going to fight on knowing the war is going to end in less than six hours?"

Aoife appeared. "Some soldiers need our help. There's some last-minute fighting going on."

Phelim looked at Seamus. "There, I told you!"

"What's happening?" I asked.

"The African-American 92nd Division are suffering heavy casualties – they need medical assistance."

"They call them the Buffalo Soldier Division after the black soldiers in the American Civil War." I said.

Seamus grinned. "I'm so proud of him. What a history expert!"

Aoife continued. "The 167th Field Artillery Brigade is part of the 92nd Division. They are stationed near the Moselle River. Let's get over there."

We didn't have to be asked twice.

As we arrived at the 167th we could see they were preparing for an attack.

"What's going on, folks?" Seamus asked one of the officers.

"I'm First Lieutenant Thompson. What do you mean

127

what's going on? We've orders to carry out a final attack on the Germans!"

"With only a few hours to go to the end of the war, why put lives at risk?" I said.

"I don't think our leaders are fully convinced about the Armistice. They think that the Germans are being given an easy way out of the war, just as the Allies are about to defeat them completely."

"Why are you going through with it?" I asked.

"It's our duty. Besides, perhaps they are right. Maybe this is just a trick by the Germans to buy more time. They have tried to be clever before," he said as he took a letter from his pocket. "Take a look at this."

"Where did you get this?" I asked.

"The Germans dropped them from the air a couple of weeks ago."

It read:

To the Colored Soldiers of the American Army –

Hello, boys, what are you doing over here? Fighting the Germans? Why? Have they ever done you any harm? Of course some white folks and the lying English-American papers told you that the Germans ought to be wiped out for the sake of Humanity and Democracy.

What is Democracy? Personal freedom, all citizens enjoying the same rights socially and before the law. Do you enjoy the same rights as the white people do

128

in America, the land of Freedom and Democracy, or are you rather not treated over there as second-class citizens? Can you go into a restaurant where white people dine? Can you get a seat in the theater where white people sit? Can you get a seat or a berth in the railroad car, or can you even ride, in the South, in the same streetcar with white people? And how about the law? Is lynching and the most horrible crimes connected therewith a lawful proceeding in a democratic country?

Now, this is all different in Germany, where they do like colored people, where they treat them as gentlemen and as white people, and quite a number of colored people have fine positions in business in Berlin and other German cities.

Why, then, fight the Germans only for the benefit of the Wall Street robbers and to protect the millions they have loaned to the British, French, and Italians? You have been made the tool of the egotistic and rapacious rich in England and in America, and there is nothing in the whole game for you but broken bones, horrible wounds, spoiled health, or death. No satisfaction whatever will you get out of this unjust war.

You have never seen Germany. So you are fools if you allow people to make you hate us. Come over and see for yourself. Let those do the fighting who make the profit out of this war. Don't allow them to use you as cannon fodder. To carry a gun in this war is not an honor, but a shame. Throw it away and come over into the German lines. You will find friends who will help you along.

"What did you do when you received this?" I asked.

"It made us even more determined, even though we know that one of our generals has made comments about us in private."

"What comments?" I asked.

"He told his officers not to eat with us, not to shake hands with us, not to talk to us, only to meet us when necessary, and not to praise us too much in front of white Americans."

"I'm sorry to hear that," I said, shaking my head in shame.

"Why are you apologising? You didn't say it! Besides, their opinions have changed since they have seen us in action. Now they can't praise us enough for our attitude to training and our spirit and enthusiasm for dangerous work."

"When does the attack begin?" Phelim asked.

"Very soon now."

"Just before the Armistice begins?"

"Orders are orders!"

We left the area disheartened. As we turned away, we were met by another soldier.

"My name's Livermore, I heard what you were

saying to the First Lieutenant. They don't realise it, but there are going to be a lot of little crosses over the graves of those lads who are going to die a useless death on this November morning."

"Isn't there anything you can do to stop it?" Aoife asked.

"Not a thing. General Pershing, the leader of the American army, sent communications to all officers that the Armistice was signed this morning. He did not tell them what they should do between then and 11a.m. It's left up to the commanding officer to decide."

"Why would he do such a thing?" Aoife asked.

"Look, you have to understand, there are two types of officers we are dealing with. One type is looking for glory and medals before the war ends, the other is looking to keep the soldiers safe until 11 a.m."

"Well, it looks like you have the first type here," Phelim muttered.

"It's not just here. Major General Summerall is in command of the V Troop. I hear he has ordered his marines to cross the Meuse River this morning."

"But the Germans will be on the other side waiting for them!" Seamus protested.

"Can't we try and stop them?" I pleaded.

"Well, you are welcome to try, but I doubt you will be successful." He produced a map and showed us their position.

As we raced over to the area, the Major General was speaking to some of his troops before battle.

"Men, we are swinging the door by its hinges. It has got to move. If we increase the pressure we can bring about the enemy's defeat."

Seamus shook his head. "What is he talking about?"

"Something about a creaky door," Phelim mumbled.

"The only thing creaky around here is his reasoning," Seamus replied.

"Get into action and get across," the Major General continued. *"I don't expect to see any of you again, but that doesn't matter. You have the honour of a definitive success – give yourself to that."*

"Stop, come back!" I shouted as I started to run towards the soldiers. Seamus grabbed me.

"We can't stop them, lad. They'll shoot you for trying."

"But he is telling them to attack an army that has already been beaten and that has surrendered!"

"There's nothing we can do, Liam!" Aoife insisted. "You cannot change what is about to happen!"

"If I could only save one, is that too much to ask?"

"Yes, I'm sorry," Aoife replied sadly.

We watched as the marines started to make temporary pontoon bridges to cross the river. German machine guns began to fire, and one by one the soldiers fell back into the water. Eventually, they successfully crossed and attacked the machine-gun areas with more loss of life. The Americans soon took control of the area. Many had been killed. We helped the wounded as best we could.

Phelim took charge. "We've done all we can here. We need to get back to our own unit."

We were able to get a lift back in an army transport. We travelled in silence after what we had witnessed.

After arriving back, Tom and I were ordered back into the trenches one last time by one of the sergeants.

"Keep watch, lads, just in case someone decides to do something silly before 11 a.m.," the sergeant said.

Tom protested. "What could possibly happen in the next few minutes, sarge? It's almost over!"

"You are still soldiers and you will follow orders. Take these rifles. You should not need them, but just in case."

Tom and I reluctantly took the guns and stood side by side in the trench. The minutes seemed to crawl by. Everything was quiet.

"Hang on a second. Who is that out there?" Tom inquired.

I looked out over the trench. A lone figure was stumbling towards our position. He was very unsteady on his feet.

Tom began to panic. *"He's coming this way! Maybe he has a grenade!"*

"It could be one of ours. He's still a long way away, Tom – besides, he can't get us from there. Here, hand me those field glasses."

The figure was slowly coming closer and closer.

I looked through the field glasses. I could not make out the uniform he was wearing. There was some blood around his stomach area.

"Whoever it is, he's been wounded. Keep your head, Tom, keep your head!"

Tom aimed his rifle. "I have him in my sights!"

Suddenly the figure started to run towards us.

"Maybe he's not injured at all! Maybe that's not his blood! He's getting closer! He has a grenade, I'm sure of it!"

"Don't shoot, Tom!"

"I'm not dying now having come this far. I'm not! It's either him or me! In a few more seconds he'll be near enough to throw a grenade!"

"If you pull that trigger it's murder, Tom, and you know it!"

"This is war, Liam. It's self-defence, not murder!"

"Don't shoot, Tom!"

Just then the bugle sounded. The Armistice had come into effect. The war was over. The men in the trenches whooped and cheered and hugged one another.

A shot rang out. The person in front of us fell to the ground.

Aoife ran to me and threw her arms about me.

"*It's over!*" she cried. "*We made it! I knew we would!*"

Tom and I looked out at the person who had just been shot.

"What's wrong?" Aoife asked.

"I could have killed him, but I didn't," Tom said nervously, pointing towards the fallen man. "I shot him in the arm."

We all jumped out and ran towards the injured person.

When we arrived, the person was groaning loudly.

Tom bent down beside him. "I'm sorry, you'll be all right. We're here now. We'll take care of you."

"Tom, go back and get Seamus and Phelim to bring the stretcher!" Aoife ordered.

"He's been shot in the arm – why is there so much blood on his body?" Aoife asked.

I ripped open the shirt which was covered in red blood. There was a large bullet hole just above his belly button.

"The wound to his arm is not serious," Aoife said. "Someone else shot him in the stomach first! We have to try and stop the bleeding!"

I took off my jacket and shirt. I rolled my shirt into a ball and pressed it on the wound to try and stem the flow of blood.

"*It's not working! The bleeding won't stop!*" I shouted.

The person's face started to turn grey.

"The wound is too deep. There's nothing we can do, Liam, I'm sorry," Aoife whispered.

"Can't we save one person, Aoife, just one? I know you have the power to do it."

"We can't change history, you know that!"

The person continued to groan in pain. His breathing became weaker.

"He's slipping away, it's now or never! Please, Aoife, I'm begging you!"

Aoife put her hands over the wound. "I should not be doing this!"

"Please!"

Aoife closed her eyes and started to concentrate. A bright purple light shot from her hands and covered the wound in an eerie glow. Within seconds the wound had disappeared.

"You did it! You did it!"

Aoife sat back, exhausted.

"Hello!" the person whispered weakly.

The grey-haired person looked vaguely familiar.

"Don't you remember me?" he asked.

"Have we met?" I asked.

"Remember that first Christmas, Button Boy?"

"Helmut? Is that you? What happened to you?"

"Listen to me carefully, Liam. The day this war started in 1914, the lights started to go out all over

Europe. Years later, the continent still lies in darkness. There is a new war now – a war against pure evil!"

"But who shot you?"

"You did!"

I was stunned. "I shot you? When?"

"1944."

Seamus and Phelim arrived with the stretcher.

"Where's Tom?" Aoife asked.

"He's in shock," Phelim replied. "A medical orderly is looking after him."

Seamus and Phelim knelt beside Helmut.

"Have we met before?" Seamus asked.

We told them what Helmut had said.

"Liam shot you?" Phelim said, looking at me accusingly.

"How did you get here?" Seamus asked suspiciously.

"I don't know. There was a young girl there who came to help me after I had been shot. She touched my hand. The next thing I knew, I was here! It was you, wasn't it?" Helmut looked directly at Aoife.

Aoife was gobsmacked. "Me? Why did I send you here?"

"I do not know!"

Seamus shook his head. "Why is everything always so complicated with you lot?"

"All I know is that it has something to do with the horse!" Helmut added. "He wants the magical horse!"

"Ferdia?" I gasped.

"Who wants Ferdia?" Aoife asked.

"Hitler!"

We all froze for a moment as the word sunk in.

Then I noticed a yellow Star of David patch on the clothes he was wearing. It had the word '*Jude*' written on it. *Jew.*

"Why are you wearing that patch?" I asked.

"To show I am Jewish," Helmut replied. "I am on the run from the Nazis. You must send me back or they will kill my family!"

"How do we do that?" Aoife asked, perplexed.

"Touch my hand again."

Aoife nodded. "All right. Close your eyes and picture yourself back in 1944 at the exact point where you met me."

"Are you sure you should be doing this?" Phelim asked.

"Grumpy Pants is right, you know," Seamus agreed. "Aren't you taking a risk that you might change history?"

Helmut closed his eyes.

"Are you ready?" Aoife asked.

"Yes, I will see you all again in the future! And remember, the horse, it's always been about the horse!"

Aoife held Helmut's hand.

He sighed. "Nothing's happening!"

Aoife shook her head. She began to get frustrated.

I reached out to pat her on the arm. "It's all right, take your time!"

In an instant there was a purple glow and Helmut disappeared.

"What happened?" Phelim asked.

Seamus jumped up and down. "That's it! You come as a pair!"

Phelim rubbed his chin. "He's right. Whatever time-travel power you have only works on other people when the two of you are in direct contact."

I smiled. "A time-travelling brother and sister? That's pretty cool!"

"Understatement of the century!" Seamus declared.

"But what about Helmut?" I asked.

"We'll have to wait 26 years to find out!" Seamus answered.

♞ ♞ ♞

Tom was well enough to leave the next day. We all reported back to headquarters for our final orders. While we were there we met the now Lieutenant-Colonel de Wiart. He was heading off to Brussels for a few days' leave.

"I'm not sure what I'm going to do with myself now," he revealed.

"You could take a trip to Ireland?" I suggested.

"I might just do that one day, when I need some peace and quiet." He sighed. "You know, I can't help thinking about all those we have lost. War is a great leveller! It shows us as we really are, not how we would like to be or how we would like other people to think of us. We are stripped of everything, with our greatness and fears all mixed together. I have fought alongside many little people who, when they were up against it, became larger than life. I will never forget them."

"No more injuries since we saw you last?" Phelim asked cheekily.

"Well, I nearly lost a leg a while back, and I got shot in the ear, but fortunately nothing too serious."

Phelim was incredulous. "Nothing too serious he says?"

Seamus laughed at Phelim. "If you cut yourself shaving, you'd be on your back for a week!"

"Well, I must be off. Perhaps we will meet again," de Wiart said.

"Perhaps. We might see you in the sequel!" Seamus joked.

"Sequel?"

"Yes, there's going to be another war!"

"I fear you may be right, if we do not handle the peace effectively!" De Wiart sighed. "Well, I'll be ready for it, if it happens!"

And with that we waved farewell for the last time.

"I suppose this is it," Tom said as we packed our kit. "I have to say I'm not going to miss the place! Are you both coming back with me?"

Aoife shook her head. "We're not going with you this time, Tom."

Tom sighed. "I'm really going to miss you all. We've been through so much. You're like family."

I hugged him tightly. "We will always be family," I whispered.

"We'll meet again," Aoife said as she hugged him too.

We said goodbye to Tom as he set off on a lorry to Calais. From there he was going to get a boat back home to Ireland.

"Will he be okay?" Aoife asked.

"Yes, he'll forget about you over the next few days and weeks as his memory of meeting us fades."

"All right. So how do we get back?"

"Close your eyes. Picture yourself back in the ward with Mum and me."

I did as I was told.

"Now, I'm going to lay my hands on your head. Ready?"

I nodded. Nothing happened.

"Have you not gone yet?" Phelim asked as he arrived with Seamus to say goodbye.

"Can't wait to get rid of me?" I laughed.

141

Phelim whacked Seamus on the shoulder. "Of course he's not gone yet. He won't go until we disappear."

"And why is that?" Seamus asked.

"Because he doesn't trust you here on your own – who knows what trouble you'd get yourself into?" Phelim joked.

The sound of the whinny of a horse came through the air.

"*Ferdia!*" I shouted.

The horse approached and nuzzled his nose against my head.

"Typical – that nag always shows up when the job is done!"

Aoife's eyes lit up. "Get on the horse, Liam!"

"What?"

"With Ferdia, our little circle is complete. We all have to be together for the magic to work on you."

I climbed up onto the saddle.

As I faced the group, the images of Seamus and Phelim began to disappear.

Seamus nodded triumphantly. "There we go – told you we had to go first!"

"I wish your mouth would go first!" Phelim said.

"See you next time, Liam!" Seamus shouted before they both vanished. Everything began to grow dark.

"*Ride, Liam, ride!*" Aoife called to me. "Ferdia knows where to take you!"

"What about you?"

"I'm in my cot in the hospital ward, remember? I'm fine! You need to go before the darkness catches up with you."

"Why? What's in the darkness?"

"It is the end of time! The darkness extinguishes everything in its wake. It is the universe's way of controlling time travel. Your task here is done. You have to leave. The universe will not let you remain. Escape now or you will be destroyed. Ferdia will take you to safety!"

"What about Helmut's message from 1944?"

"I don't know! We'll have to work that out another time! Now ride! I'll see you on the other side. *Go, Ferdia!*"

Ferdia began to gallop off at a pace so fast I could hardly hang on. As I looked behind the darkness soon surrounded Aoife and she could no longer be seen.

The scenery whizzed by as the darkness seemed to get closer and closer.

"Faster, Ferdia, faster! The darkness is closing in! Go! Go!"

Just as we were about to be swallowed up we reached the French coast and the chalky white cliffs of Étretat.

"Whoa, Ferdia, whoa!"

Ferdia leaped off the cliff. I hung onto his neck with all of the strength I could muster. I could see the water loom before me.

I closed my eyes and braced for impact . . . which is where this story began.

Chapter 11

Present Day: Back To the Present

So now, you're up to date!

Just as I was expecting to hit the water, I heard a voice I recognised.

"Liam, Liam! Are you all right?"

It was my mother's voice!

I opened my eyes and adjusted to the light. "Mum? Mum!" I reached out to hug her.

"Oh, you did give me a scare!"

I looked at the cot. "Is Aoife all right?"

"She's fine! How about you? When I came back from the bathroom you were by the cot, almost in a daze!"

"How long have I been like this?"

"Well, I was only gone for a few minutes."

"Is that all?"

"Yes, why?"

"Oh, no reason."

"How are you feeling?"

"Fine, I think I'm getting used to it."

"Getting used to what, darling?"

"Oh, nothing!" I said. "Mum, do me a favour. Touch my hand for a moment."

"You want me to touch your hand?"

"Yes!"

"Of course I will! Now what?"

"Think back to that night in 1988 when you saw Great-grandfather Tom for the last time."

"Liam, are you sure you're all right?" Mum touched my brow to check for a temperature.

"Yes!"

"All right, this seems a bit strange, but I'll play along."

I closed my eyes and concentrated. I touched Aoife's hand at the same time. The room began to change shape.

In a matter of seconds a grown Aoife and I appeared back in 1988 in Tom's bedroom, the night he died. He was asleep in his bed.

"It's definitely him all right," I whispered.

"Are you sure?" Aoife asked.

"I may be older and greyer, but there's nothing wrong with my hearing! Show yourselves!" Tom called out as he turned on his bedside lamp.

We stood closer to the bed so that we could be seen.

"Can you see us?" Aoife asked.

"Not so well. My eyes aren't what they used to be. But I recognise your voices!"

"How do you remember us?" I said.

"You were always there at the back of my mind. I knew you would come back one day." He squinted. "You look younger than before! How is that possible? Are you angels?"

"No, we're your family!" I replied. "From the future! You're seeing us as twelve-year-olds!" I held Tom's hand. "I want you to know that the story of your life and your part in the Great War will never be forgotten. We will make sure of that. You won't be the unknown soldier anymore."

A tear came to his eye.

"Thank you. They don't believe me, you know, apart from Geri."

"Geri? You mean Geraldine? That's our mum!" I said.

"We will never forget," Aoife repeated as she went to hold Tom's other hand.

"Thank you," he whispered. "That is such a relief."

"Sleep now, Tom," I whispered.

Tom's breathing started to become shallower. He closed his eyes.

"Thank you," he murmured, "thank you for coming back to me one last time ..."

Aoife hugged him and kissed him on his forehead. Then she took my hand in hers.

146

"He's gone, Liam."

"*Where's he gone?*" a voice shouted.

I looked up. I was back on the hospital bed holding my mother's hand. Only a few seconds had passed in real time.

"*There he is!*" said a voice from the door.

It was my old gang, back again for another visit.

"Why is your face wet, Liam? Were you crying?" Pat smirked.

"*Pat!*" Nuala hissed.

"*Ouch!* What's that for!" he said, rubbing his arm.

"That's for being an insensitive dope!" Nuala replied. "I'll pinch you again if you don't watch it!"

"How's the history project going?" I asked, wiping the tears from my eyes.

Pat groaned. "So much information! So many books! So many words!"

Mikhail wheeled his wheelchair closer to me and produced a large book.

"Look at this one, Liam. I got it from the library. This is a really good one, look. Pat, you should like it – *not too many words!*"

Pat shrugged. "Words are overrated."

"Well, try using less of them," Nuala retorted.

Sanjay held out his hand. "Let's see that, Mikhail." He started to flick through the pages. "Look at all these pictures of Indian soldiers who fought in the war!"

"And the pictures of the women who kept the factories going and acted as nurses on the front while the men went off to fight," Nuala added.

Pat looked as if he was going to say something smart but he stopped short. He grabbed the book for himself and flicked through the pages.

"Look, there's a picture of three German soldiers and a dog!" Pat cried. "Three soldiers ... Bavarian regiment ... dog called Fuchsi ... pit bull ... it says the dog was a stray and was trained to do circus tricks. Fancy that!"

He held up the book and we all gazed at the photograph.

"Can I see the picture, Pat?" I said. "One of those faces looks familiar."

Pat handed me the book so that I could see more clearly.

As I looked at the picture I focused on the soldier on the right, the tall one with the moustache. I had seen him before. I recognised him from the Battle of the Somme. It was the German despatcher who ran away when I pointed my rifle at him.

"I don't suppose it gives the name of that soldier on the right, does it?"

Pat squinted.

"Just the initials 'A.H.'"

"Is that all?"

"Yup. Haven't a clue, could be anyone. *Ouch!* Nuala, why did you pinch me again? I didn't do anything."

Nuala was seething.

"A.H. – ring a bell?"

"Amorphous Hippotamus?" Pat suggested.

"Adolf Hitler!" Mikhail shouted.

"Adolf Hitler?" I repeated as my head started to spin. The voices suddenly became quite distant.

"No, it can't be!" I insisted. "He looks quite different in the photograph."

"His moustache is longer and he's younger and thinner, but that's definitely him."

I kept playing back the scenario in my mind. I had Adolf Hitler in my sights and I let him go. Could I have done something? Could I have changed the path of history? The words of Aoife came back to me: "You cannot change what has already happened – you cannot interfere." And yet, the question persisted. Could I have stopped Hitler? Could I have made a difference?

"You have made a difference, Liam," I heard a voice whisper.

I looked around. "What?"

"Liam, are you all right?" Sanjay asked, concerned.

I nodded my head. "Yes, I think so, thanks, Sanjay – just something that didn't agree with me, I think."

Pat piped up. "I know how that feels. Nuala never agrees with me!" He stepped away before Nuala's nails could make contact with his arm.

As the conversation continued, I looked at Mum who

was now feeding Aoife. We'd had a lucky escape in our latest adventure, that was for sure. I had met some interesting and brave people like Major Bridges, Captain Amos, Nurse Edith Cavell, Captain Adrian Carton de Wiart and the poet Francis Ledwidge. I would never forget them. The images of pain and suffering were burned into my brain, and yet with that there was also a sense of hope. We had kept Tom safe. We had saved Helmut's life. Was there still one adventure to be had as Helmut predicted? Would our third adventure turn out to be third time lucky?

"That's funny," Nuala remarked, snapping me back to reality.

"What is?" I asked.

"That picture of Hitler – I just noticed."

"What's that?"

"The horse?"

I froze. "Horse?"

"Yes, there in the background – you can almost only see it out of the corner of your eye. There's a horse standing behind Hitler. How did I miss that?"

I looked closely. It was Ferdia. The words came back to me: *"The horse, it's always been about the horse."*

The words still did not make sense to me but something told me one person had the answers to all of this – Adolf Hitler.

I looked into Baby Aoife's eyes.

"Well, Aoife," I said. "I think we have one more journey to make. Are you ready?"

Aoife's eyes seemed to sparkle as I touched her hand. The people in the room started to fade as the room went very bright.

"Here we go again, Aoife!" I shouted. *"Hold on tight!"*

The End

Coming Next – The Concluding Part of the *Liam and Aoife Trilogy (Hands on History: My Time)*
Operation Valkyrie – The Plot to Kill Hitler
Liam and Aoife's Third and Final Adventure

Afterword

Ireland and the First World War

Over 200,000 Irish people fought in the war which was widely supported by the people of Ireland. Most fought in the British army. Others joined the navy or air force, or served with the armies of Canada, Australia, New Zealand or South Africa. The actual number of Irish who died in the war is uncertain. It is thought that about 35,000 died, although this number could be higher.

At the time Ireland was split between Nationalists, led by John Redmond who wanted Home Rule, and Unionists, led by Edward Carson, who wanted Ireland to continue to be governed as part of the United Kingdom. Nationalists and Unionists fought together during the war. The Easter Rising in 1916 and a failed attempt by Britain to force conscription in Ireland in 1918 brought about a change of opinion amongst

Nationalists. Irish soldiers who came back from the war were ignored and forgotten. Many were also suffering from Post-Traumatic Stress Disorder. Home Rule was no longer enough. The Irish Parliamentary Party was wiped out by Sinn Féin at the general election in 1918.

There was no formal monument to the Irish soldiers who had lost their lives in the war until 1988 when the Irish National War Memorial Gardens in Dublin were opened.

The Treaty of Versailles and its Aftermath

After a war which had seen the death of over 20 million people, the Treaty of Versailles was signed on 28th June 1919. This marked the official end to hostilities. France wanted to make sure that Germany would never be strong enough again to wage a war while Britain and the United States of America did not want to give German any reason for going to war again. The League of Nations, an early version of the United Nations was created.

Germany had to hand over parts of its territory to other countries. It also lost all of its colonies in China, the Pacific and Africa. It had to agree to have a smaller army and had to pay damages for "being the aggressor". Germany, now a republic (known as the Weimar Republic) signed the treaty under protest as it had believed it would not be punished so harshly. The treaty also changed the borders of Europe and split the Austro-Hungarian Empire into countries such as Yugoslavia, Poland and Czechoslovakia.

Some Germans felt betrayed by the politicians who signed the treaty. This later helped the Nazi party come to power under Adolf Hitler as they promised to reverse the treaty and make Germany great again. There is a view among some historians that the Versailles Treaty made the Second World War inevitable due to its harsh treatment of Germany. Others believe that while it certainly played a part, it was not the only reason war broke out again in 1939.

Historical Notes

Allied Powers

The main Allied Powers consisted of Britain, France, Russia, Japan, Italy and the United States.

Assassination of Archduke Ferdinand and his wife Sophie

The Archduke and his wife actually avoided a previous attempt on their lives earlier that same day, 28th June, 1914, in Sarajevo. Instead of leaving after the failed attempt they decided to visit someone in hospital who had been injured in the attack. The car they were travelling in took a wrong turn and stopped right beside one of the original assassins, 19-year old Gavrilo Princip who could not believe his luck. He shot both the Archduke and his wife at close range, killing them instantly. It was the shots that changed the history of the world and cost the lives of millions in a world war. Princip later expressed regret for the shooting of Sophie and died in jail in 1918.

Captain Arthur Moore O'Sullivan (Amos)

Captain O'Sullivan was born in India in 1879 where his father worked as an advocate general. He eventually ended up living in Greystones, Co. Wicklow. He fired the shot that ended the Christmas truce at Neuve Chapelle in December 1914. He was injured in March 1915. He died at the Battle of Aubers Ridge in May 1915 and is buried in the Royal Irish Rifles graveyard at Laventie, France.

Captain Adrian Carton de Wiart

Pictured on the cover of this book, Captain de Wiart, half-Irish, half-Belgian, was born in 1880 in Belgium. He was a career soldier who fought in the Boer War and both world wars. He suffered injuries to his face, head, stomach, ankle, leg, hip and ear. He also survived plane crashes and escaped from a prison-of-war camp during the Second World War. He became a Lieutenant-General in the army. He was also a close friend of British Prime Minister Winston Churchill and was knighted, becoming Sir Adrian Carton de Wiart. He spent his last years living in County Cork. He died in 1963, aged 83, and is buried at Killinardish Churchyard, Carrigadrohid, County Cork.

Captain George K Livermore

Captain Livermore was the operations officer of the 167th Field Artillery Brigade of the Black 92nd Division. He tried unsuccessfully to stop the attacks before the official 11 a.m. ceasefire. He later wrote a letter to his local US congressman stating that lives had been unnecessarily lost in the final hours of the war.

Central Powers

The main Central Powers were made up of Germany, Austria-Hungary, the Ottoman Empire and Bulgaria.

Edward Carson

Carson was a leader of the Irish Unionist Alliance and the Ulster Unionist Party between 1910 and 1921. He campaigned against Home Rule and helped to establish the Ulster Volunteers to fight against it, if necessary. When Home Rule was postponed in 1914 after the outbreak of war, many of these volunteers went to fight in the war as part of the 36th (Ulster) Division. Carson was made First Lord of the Admiralty in 1916 and was part of the War Cabinet between 1917 and 1918. After the war he argued for the six Ulster counties to be exempt from any possible Home Rule agreement. He turned down the chance to become the first Prime Minister of Northern Ireland. When he died in 1935, he was given a state funeral.

Edith Cavell

Edith Cavell was born in 1865 in Norfolk, England. She became a nurse and was based in Belgium when war broke out. She believed in treating all injured no matter what country they fought for. She was arrested by the Germans for helping hundreds of Allied soldiers escape from German-occupied Belgium. She was found guilty in a military court and shot by firing squad in October, 1915, despite worldwide protests. Her body was returned to England in 1919 and buried at Norwich Cathedral after a memorial service at Westminster Abbey. Some of her final words were *"I must have no hatred or bitterness towards anyone."*

Francis Ledwidge

Francie Ledwidge wrote over 120 poems. He was born in Slane, County Meath, in 1887, and the cottage he was born in is now the Francis Ledwidge Museum. He joined the Royal Inniskilling Fusiliers and served at Gallipoli. After the Easter Rising in 1916 and the execution of his close friend and fellow poet Thomas MacDonagh, he questioned his role in the British Army. He was killed on 31st July 1917 when a shell exploded on a road which he was repairing. He is buried in Artillery Wood Military Cemetery. In 1998 a memorial was unveiled at the exact spot where he died.

General John J. Pershing

Leader of the American army and regarded as a war hero, Pershing was promoted to General of the Armies, the highest rank in the army, after the war. There was some controversy over his decision not to cease fighting after Germany agreed to surrender. Over 3,500 American soldiers were killed or injured on 11th November between the hours of 5 a.m (when the armistice was signed) and 11 a.m. (the official end of the war).

Home Rule

The right of Irish people to govern themselves while remaining part of the United Kingdom.

"It's a Long Way to Tipperary"

This was written in 1912 by Henry Williams and Jack Judge. It became popular among soldiers in the war and is still well known today.

"John"

Aoife called herself "John" in the story. This was inspired by the story of Private John Condon from Waterford who died at the age of 14 in a gas attack at the Second Battle of Ypres in 1915. This makes him the youngest soldier to die in the war. He is buried at Poelcapelle Cemetry in Flanders. A bronze memorial can be found in Cathedral Square, Waterford. Incidentally, the oldest person to die in the war was 82-year-old Field Marshall Frederick Lord Roberts, the Earl of Waterford. It is said that the phrase "Bob's your uncle" is associated with the Earl due to his popularity with the troops.

John Redmond

Redmond was the leader of the Irish Parliamentary Party from 1900 until 1918. He gave a famous speech on 20th September, 1914, in Woodenbridge, County Wicklow, where he encouraged Irishmen to "do their duty" and defend "the highest principles of religion and morality and right". He believed that Nationalists and Unionists should fight together to help Britain win the war and that this would improve relations between both. As a result up to 200,000 Irish Nationalists joined the army, including his own brother, Willie, who died in the war. The Easter Rising in 1916 came as a surprise to him. By 1918, when support for Home Rule and Redmond was waning, a dejected Redmond died on 6th March after suffering heart failure. His party lost most of its parliamentary seats to Sinn Féin in the 1918 general election.

Major Tom Bridges

Major Bridges did indeed use a tin whistle and a toy drum to rally the troops in Saint-Quentin. He lost a leg in battle in 1917 and in later years became the Governor of South Australia.

No Man's Land

This term was used to describe the area between the trenches of the warring armies.

Ringo Starr

Real-name Richard Starkey, Ringo was the drummer of one of the most popular and successful bands of all time – The Beatles. His fellow band members were Paul McCartney, John Lennon and George Harrison. He still releases songs, and tours with his own band around the world.

Roger Casement

Born in 1864, Casement was a diplomat who worked to improve human rights in the Congo and Peru. He was knighted in 1911 and was arrested in 1916 for trying to get weapons from Germany to support the rebels in the Easter Rising. Despite appeals from Sir Arthur Conan Doyle (creator of Sherlock Holmes), the poet W.B. Yeats, the playwright George Bernard Shaw and the United States Senate, Casement was executed on 3rd August 1916. His remains were sent back to Ireland in 1965 where he was given a state funeral. He is buried at Glasnevin Cemetery.

Russian Revolution

The people of Russia revolted against its ruler, Tsar

Nicholas II, in 1917. At this stage over 2 million Russians had been killed in the war and almost 5 million wounded. The army refused to fire on the population who were protesting, and the Tsar had to give up his throne. The Bolsheviks led by Vladimir Lenin eventually took control in October 1917 and signed a peace treaty with Germany which took Russia out of the war in March 1918.

Shell Shock (Post-Traumatic Stress Disorder)

Over 300 British and Commonwealth soldiers were executed for cowardice or desertion. Soldiers from other armies were also executed for the same offences. In many of these cases the soldiers were young men who were suffering from what we now call post-traumatic stress disorder. It was referred to as "shell shock" at the time. Post-traumatic stress disorder is a mental health condition that can occur when a person has been exposed to a traumatic (deeply disturbing) event, such as warfare. In 2007, justice was finally seen to be done for these young men when they were officially pardoned by the British government. Over 80,000 soldiers were treated for "shell shock" during the war. Many thousands were still being treated years after the war had ended.

Star of David

The Star of David is a six-pointed star that has become a symbol of Jewish identity. It can be found on the flag of Israel.

Tuberculosis

This is an infectious disease caused by bacteria in the lungs. While the BCG vaccine is available to prevent the disease, over a million people worldwide still die from this infection.

Discussion Questions

1. What did you know about the war before you read this book?

2. If you had an opinion about the war before you read this book, has this view now changed? Why/Why not?

3. Why did so many countries go to war with one another?

4. In your opinion, could war have been avoided?

5. Why did so many Irish fight in the British Army?

6. Do you have any family members who fought in the First World War?

7. Where could you go to find out information about the war?

8. Does it surprise you to hear that the soldiers got together in Christmas 1914 to share treats and play football?

9. Why did soldiers from India fight in the war?

10. Did you know that Adolf Hitler fought in the First World War?

11. Why were there so many rats in the trenches?

12. Why did it take the USA so long to enter the war?

13. What happened to Germany after the war?

14. Have you ever been to a war museum? What have you seen?

15. Do you know that there is a war memorial in Dublin Connolly Train Station? People walk by it every day and do not notice. It is on the wall of Platform 4 beside the drinks and snacks machine. The next time you go to the station, see if you can find it.

Timeline

1914

29th *April* – Archduke Ferdinand and his wife Sophie assassinated.

28th *July* – The Austro-Hungarian Empire declares war on Serbia.

1st *August* – Germany declares war on Russia.

3rd *August* – Germany declares war on France. German army invades Belgium.

4th *August* – Britain declares war on Germany.

13th *August* – Japan declares war on Germany.

29th *October* – Turkey enters the war.

2nd *November* – Russia declares war on Turkey.

5th *November* – Britain and France declare war on Turkey.

Late 1914 – German army marches into France. Stopped at Marne and the 1st Battle of Ypres.

1915

2nd *April* – 2nd Battle of Ypres. Poison gas used for the first time.

7th *May* – *Lusitania* sunk by a German U-Boat.

23rd *May* – Italy enters the war

September – The first tank "Little Willie" is produced for use in the war by Britain.

October – The British navy attack at the Dardanelles fails. Winston Churchill, First Lord of the Admiralty, resigns.

1916

February to November – The Battle of Verdun. 540,000 French soldiers killed. 430,000 German soldiers killed.

April – Romania enters the war.

31st May – The Battle of Jutland. This is the only large naval battle to take place during the war between Britain and Germany. Both sides claim victory.

July to November – Battle of the Somme. 60,000 in the British Army are killed on the first day of battle – 420,000 in total are killed. Another 200,000 French soldiers and 500,000 German soldiers are killed.

1917

January – The Zimmerman telegram is sent proposing an alliance between Mexico and Germany.

6th April – USA declares war on Germany.

November – Russian Bolshevik revolution.

December – Russia ends the war with Germany.

1918

August – Bulgaria surrenders.

October – Allied forces control most of France and part of Belgium. Turkey surrenders.

November – The Hindenburg Line collapses. Kaiser Wilhelm abdicates.

11th November – The war ends.

1919

28th June – The Treaty of Versailles is signed.

1921

Matthias Erzberger, Germany Minister of Finance who signed the Treaty of Versailles, is assassinated by a right-wing group.

1922

Walther Rathenau, German Foreign Minister, shot and killed with a machine gun by a right-wing group.

1923

"The Beer Hall Putsch" – Adolf Hitler attempts to overthrow the local Bavarian government in Germany. The attempt begins in a beer hall. It fails and Hitler is sent to prison.

1929

The American stock market crashes. Major banks collapse and millions lose their jobs all over the world. The German economy suffers.

1930

The Nazi Party wins almost 20% of the vote in German elections.

1933

Adolf Hitler, leader of the Nazi Party, becomes Chancellor (Prime Minister) of Germany.

1939

World War II begins after Hitler's Germany invades Poland.

Acknowledgements

Eleven books later (!) my thanks again go to Paula Campbell in Poolbeg Press and the rest of the team – Kieran, Caroline, Dave, Lee, Orla, Andy, Ron and Conor. Thanks also to Gaye Shortland, my editor, who continues to advise, encourage and cajole where necessary!

Hats off also to the very talented designer Derry Dillon whose illustrations have brought my various characters to life over the years.

And thanks to Sara Dooley, aged 14, for her fantastic map-illustration. Sara, you have a wonderful talent!

Thanks to Denise, Alex and Oisín for their continuous support. Thanks to Nuala and Jean for being such good neighbours!

Thanks to Jasmine O'Brien, Pat O'Brien, Denise Rafferty and Tony Dooley for reviewing the drafts of this book and providing feedback. Thanks too to Zara O'Brien for her words of encouragement. Keep on running, Zara!

A word of thanks to everyone at Fingal Libraries, Children's Books Ireland, Writing.ie. Irish Writing Centre, Dublin Book Festival, Hays Festival, Tara Book Company, Karin Ennis, Canada Life Europe and the Irish

Life Group who have always given me encouragement to follow my dream to write.

Thanks to John Manning in the *Fingal Independent/Drogheda Independent* who continues to feature me in articles – much obliged!

A word of thanks again to Cyril Gillen and my old school St. Joseph's Drogheda, who have a photo of me on their wall (I hope it's a small photo – I don't want to scare the students!).

A special mention to Jenny Mangan, Librarian, and the young people involved in the Creative Writing Group at Larkin Community College in Dublin. Some of you have now been involved in the group for the last three years. Where did those years go? I hope those of you who did the Junior Cycle got through it all right! See you all again soon! Let's do a few school writing trips this year with Jenny!

Finally, I promised Mark and Mya Smith, Mark Stanley and Erik Bakken I would say hello to them in my next book, so hello there, folks! I also promised the students of St. Mochta's in Clonsilla that I would give them a shout-out – so "HELLO! HELLO!" to you all.

Thank you for taking the time to read this book. I have done my best to get my historical facts correct. I hope I have done justice to the subject matter. There was so much more I wanted to put in this book, but there just was not enough room. I hope this book encourages you to find out more about this topic. This terrible war had a huge impact on Ireland and the world that we should try to remember. When we forget our history, we forget an important part of ourselves.

Well done!

For those children who have managed to read this far, I say "Well done!" As a reward, I will send the first 5 children who contact Poolbeg Books a selection of my books. Simply send a postcard or a note to Poolbeg Press, Baldoyle, Dublin 13, telling me what you liked (or didn't like!) about the book. Don't forget to include your address. Thanks again and I hope to see you all next time for the third and final story in the Liam and Aoife trilogy.

Books and Articles Referenced

This list is not exhaustive but provides a good representation of the books and articles referenced while researching the subject matter of this book.

Connelly, C. *The Forgotten Soldier – The True Story of an Ordinary Boy who fought and fell in the Great War.* HarperElement. London. 2014.

Cornish, P. T*he First World War Galleries.* Imperial War Museum. London. 2014.

Cowsill, A. *World War One, 1914 – 1918. A Graphic Novel.* Kalyani Navyug Media Pvt Ltd. New Delhi, India. 2014. (Illustrator: Lalit Kumar Sharma.)

Desagneaux, Henri. *A French Soldier's Diary 1914-1918.* Pen & Sword Military. Barnsley. 1975.

De Wiart, A. C. Lieutenant-General. *Happy Odyssey.* Pen & Sword Military. Barnsley. 1950.

Emden, R. *Temporary Heroes – Lieutenant Norman Cecil Down.* Pen & Sword Military. Barnsley. 2014. (Originally published 1917.)

Emden, R. *Teenage Tommy – Memoirs of a Cavalryman in the First World War.* Pen & Sword Military. Barnsley. 2013.

Gleeson, Joe. *Irish Aces of the RFC and RAF in the First World War – The Lives Behind the Legends.* Fonthill Media Limited. United Kingdom. 2015.

Jervis, H.S. Lieutenant-Colonel. *The 2nd Munsters in France.* Naval & Military Press. East Sussex. 1922.

Remarque, E. M. *All Quiet on the Western Front.* Vintage Books. London. 1994 (Translated from German. Originally published in 1929.)

Scotland, T. and Heys, S. *Understanding the Somme 1916 – An Illuminating Battlefield Guide.* Helion and Company. Solihull. 2017.

Taylor, A.J.P. *An Illustrated History of The First World War.* Penguin Books. London. 1966.

Websites Referenced

The Archduke Ferdinand's Wrong Turn
https://www.history.com/news/how-a-wrong-turn-started-world-war-i

John Redmond's Speech at Woodenbridge
https://www.historyireland.com/volume-22/john-redmonds-woodenbridge-speech/

Military Cemeteries from World War I
https://www.ww1cemeteries.com/

The Christmas 1914 Truce
https://www.irishtimes.com/culture/heritage/1914-christmas-truce-all-quiet-on-the-western-front-as-guns-were-silenced-1.2047017

American World War I Archives
https://www.archives.gov/research/genealogy/wwi

War Graves Commission
www.cwgc.org

Post-Traumatic Stress and the First World War – Tim Field
https://bullyonline.org/old/stress/ww1.htm

Shell Shock during World War One
https://www.bbc.co.uk/history/worldwars/wwone/shellshock_01.shtml

Edith Cavell
https://edithcavell.org.uk/

Irish War Memorials
http://www.irishwarmemorials.ie/

Connolly Station War Memorial – Platform 4
http://www.irishwarmemorials.ie/Memorials-Detail?memoId=165

World War 1: Wasted Lives on Armistice Day
https://www.historynet.com/world-war-i-wasted-lives-on-armistice-day.htm

Some Museums Worth a Visit
Collins Barracks, Arbour Hill, Dublin 7.
https://www.museum.ie/Decorative-Arts-History

Francis Ledwidge Museum
http://www.francisledwidge.com/

Irish Military War Museum, Collon, Co. Meath.
https://www.irishmilitarywarmuseum.com

The *Lusitania* Museum and Signal Tower, Old Head of Kinsale, Co. Cork.
https://www.oldheadofkinsale.com/

The Somme Museum, Conlig (between Newtownards and Bangor), Co. Down, Northern Ireland. (Ask for Andy!)
http://www.sommeassociation.com/about/somme-museum